ONE NIGHT
WITH HER
MILLIONAIRE
BOSS

ONE NIGHT WITH HER MILLIONAIRE BOSS

KANDY SHEPHERD

MILLS & BOON

First published in Great Britain 2020
by Mills & Boon, an imprint of HarperCollins*Publishers*
1 London Bridge Street, London, SE1 9GF

Large Print edition 2020

© 2020 Kandy Shepherd

ISBN: 978-0-263-08485-6

MIX
Paper from
responsible sources
FSC™ C007454

This book is produced from independently certified
FSC™ paper to ensure responsible forest management. For
more information visit www.harpercollins.co.uk/green.

Printed and bound in Great Britain
by CPI Group (UK) Ltd, Croydon, CR0 4YY

To my wonderful, clever
and patient editor, Victoria Britton,
who helps make my stories
the best they can be. Thank you!

CHAPTER ONE

NED HUDSON HAD lost count of the times he'd been best man or groomsman for one of his friends. His cousin, Erin, however—one of the bridesmaids in today's ceremony—delighted in reminding him of the specifics of his track record. 'You know what they say, Ned: *five times a groomsman, never a groom,*' she teased before the service in the country town church where generations of his family had taken their vows, been christened, even buried.

Ned tried to laugh it off. 'You make it sound like a curse. Doesn't that saying apply to bridesmaids? Girls, not guys?'

'I can't see why it doesn't apply to men too,' she said. 'You're pushing thirty, Ned. Handsome, wealthy, a great guy. I don't know why you're so determined to stay single. Maybe it's time for the farmer to think about taking a wife.'

Ned gritted his teeth. He wasn't actively avoiding marriage. Far from it. He wanted a wife to share his life on Five and a Half Mile Creek, the historic homestead and vast holdings of land that had been in his family for more than one hundred and fifty years, and which was now in his hands. *Farmer* wasn't really the right word to describe him though— he was more of a CEO of a multi-faceted rural enterprise with a turnover in the multi-millions. It wasn't a role for a single guy. He needed a supportive spouse by his side. And then there was the matter of providing an heir.

But he fell for the wrong kind of women. Women who valued the trappings of his considerable wealth—the penthouse in the most exclusive part of the big city of Melbourne, the private plane, international travel—over the idea of a settled family life. Women who wanted the excitement of the city over the more fulfilling pace of the rural life he loved, but who pretended to like the country until they had him snared. Three years ago he'd fallen head over heels in love with such a woman, had come close to proposing to her, so close he'd been gutted when she'd revealed her true colours. He wouldn't get caught like that again.

Today, his brother Wil was marrying lovely Georgia. They'd been friends at university but never more than friends until Wil had taken custody of his baby daughter, Nina, after his ex-wife had died in an accident. Learning to look after the daughter Wil hadn't known about had brought him and Georgia closer and they had fallen in love.

Love. *Huh.* Wil and Georgia had been lucky in the love stakes. Ned, however, had been working on the wrong criteria when it came to relationships. The roller-coaster ride of infatuation and emotion did not appear to work for the kind of wife required for the boss of Five and a Half Mile Creek. He had seen the way it had torn his parents apart, so he should have known better. It had been a painful lesson to learn.

Never a groom. The curse-like phrase kept reverberating through his mind. He would turn thirty in a few months, and was fed up with putting his personal life on hold. Sooner rather than later, he wanted to get married, to exchange vows at this very altar. And he didn't want to deal with time-wasters like Leanne, the gold-digger who had broken his heart.

So what did he want in a wife?

As the ceremony proceeded, Ned thought about his requirements for the ideal wife and mother of his children. It didn't take him long to formulate a wish-list.

She should be tall, as he was six foot three. Dark-haired, brown-eyed women were his 'type' though he was open to hair colour, eye colour, et cetera.

But there were other, non-negotiable attributes for the future Mrs Ned Hudson:

1. Genuine enjoyment of country life essential.
2. Management experience to help run the business would be advantageous. Accountant or lawyer ideal.
3. Love of animals, particularly horses. A vet or vet nurse would be very welcome.
4. An interest in gardening.
5. A good cook.
6. Conservative, country-focused values.

But how to find her? Living out here, nearly four hundred kilometres from Melbourne, meant he couldn't count on happenstance to deliver him the right kind of wife. That meant a dating site.

He dreaded having to create a profile to sell himself. *Tall, well built, financially secure...* That might work. He was an expert horseman. Piloted his own plane. Liked reading political thrillers in his rare downtime. But above all, he was a man of the land—*his land.*

He never wanted to live anywhere else. His connection to the land came before everything. Any future wife would have to understand that. Five and a Half Mile Creek was more a vocation than a job—he'd been born to it.

He'd been an only child until he was fourteen. Then Wil, aged thirteen, had come to Five and a Half Mile Creek—a troubled foster child, hostile and hurting. Ned had treated the boy with caution and respect, as he did the lost and injured animals he cared for, and had been overjoyed when Wil had been adopted and become his brother.

His parents treated them equally as sons. However, while Wil loved Five and a Half Mile Creek, he had no desire to own it. Ned was destined to inherit the property but when his mother had survived breast cancer, his parents had decided to fulfil her bucket list by travelling around the world. Ned had been in partnership with his dad running Five and a Half Mile Creek before. Now the responsibility was entirely on his shoulders. That left little opportunity to look for a wife.

Never a groom.

By the time the reception at the homestead was in full swing, he'd decided he would not let that happen. A dating site it would have to be. After he'd posed for the last of the seemingly interminable photos where the best man was required, he managed to get away from the celebration and into his private study. No one would miss him for ten minutes or so. He closed the door, sat down at his computer and typed up that wife wish-list.

Perhaps it seemed a tad impersonal, he thought uncomfortably when he reviewed the list. In fact, it read more like an employment ad. But anyone marrying him would have to take on not just a husband but Five and a Half Mile Creek too.

Besides, there was nothing wrong with being practical. He'd fallen head over heels in love before and it hadn't worked out. In fact, each time had ended disastrously. Infatuation was *not* the basis for a lasting relationship. Practicality was the way to go. Mutual values, shared interests, a judicious getting-to-know-each-other period. That was how it could work.

He would make sure of it.

With a sigh of relief, Freya Delaney swung her little purple van into the driveway that led from an imposing set of gates to the Hudson family's historic property, Five and a Half Mile Creek. She hadn't realised just how far away from the city it was when she'd set off from Melbourne the day before. She'd actually crossed the border from the state of Victoria into New South Wales.

This was the real Australian countryside— huge skies, mile after mile of emptiness with only the occasional dwelling. Swathes of rich, productive land were devoted to crops or sheep, interspersed with areas of natural bushland.

She shuddered. How could anyone live in such isolation? The inner city with crowded, buzzing streets and a coffee shop on every corner was more to her taste.

But the landscape was beautiful in its own way and she was glad for the opportunity to visit. Not only was she on assignment for her boss, Hugh Tran, the photographer who had shot the wedding held at Five and a Half Mile Creek the previous weekend, but she was also on a secret, personal mission of her own.

She'd known Wil Hudson—though his name hadn't been Hudson then and her name hadn't been Freya—when they'd both been thirteen and in foster care. Wil had proved a true friend to her when her safety had been threatened. But she hadn't seen him since. Helping her boss edit the wedding shoot, she'd immediately recognised the handsome, dark-haired groom as grown-up Wil.

She'd felt an immense rush of relief that he'd found happiness with a lovely wife and a sweet baby daughter. Things had, thank heaven, turned out well for Wil. But she hadn't shared any of those thoughts with her boss, Hugh. All she'd done was comment on what a beautiful wedding it was. And what an utterly gorgeous location.

'I'm an old friend of Jackie Hudson, the mother of the groom,' Hugh had said. 'She was a well-known interior designer in her day—I first knew her as Jacqueline Travis. She asked me at the wedding could I photograph the newly redecorated homestead. It's a job right up your alley, Freya, would be a good thing for your portfolio. Why don't you take over the shoot?'

A shiver of what she wasn't sure was excitement or trepidation had run up her spine. 'But won't your friend expect you to do it?'

'I shot the wedding purely as a favour. Besides, Jackie doesn't live there any more. Her older son, Ned, is running the place. Good, steady kind of guy.'

Boring kind of guy, Freya translated.

She dated creative, interesting men—much good that they had done her. Her last relationship had been with a rock musician. She'd thought he'd sung to her soul, but in truth he was manipulative and borderline abusive. Freya been left with a bruised heart and hadn't let down her barriers to a man since.

She knew she should say no to the assignment. Wil had found the happy life he deserved. Freya had made something of herself too. Her traumatic past was something to be pushed to the furthest corners of her mind. She had no desire to intrude on Wil's new life. But she loved shooting interiors. And she couldn't deny she was curious about the home her old friend had ended up with after those awful years in foster care and institutions. She'd like to see Five and a Half Mile Creek.

'I'll check with her son to see if it's okay,' she'd said. 'Show me which one he is in the wedding photos.'

She'd flicked through the images of Ned Hudson, the best man. He was good-looking in a rugged, manly way—tall, wore a tux well. Even in the photos, he seemed to have a presence, as if people would take note of what he had to say. He didn't look anything like Wil but, of course, they weren't related by blood.

She'd felt some trepidation about informing Ned Hudson she was replacing his mother's choice of photographer. But when she'd called him, and had a brief, to-the-point conversation, he'd raised no objections. So here she was, ten days after the wedding, at one of the grandest pastoral properties in the country—owned by people who were in the highest echelons of society.

She drove slowly up the long, tree-lined driveway to the house, set in what must be an acre of glorious, well-tended gardens bright with autumnal colour in the early morning sun. It was more mansion than farmhouse, an imposing Victorian-era building with peaked slate roofs and turrets and surrounded on all sides by wide verandas.

She'd seen the wedding photos, but still she was knocked out by the house's classic beauty and elegance. This was serious money. *Old money.* But she wasn't intimidated. She'd shot interiors in some of the finest homes in Melbourne for the glossiest of lifestyle magazines. She could do this one justice.

Freya negotiated the circular gravel driveway and parked the van as close as she could to the house. She swung herself out of the driver's seat, to be greeted by crisp morning air, the scent of roses…and the furious barking of a dog.

The black-and-white border collie stood on

the wide veranda just steps away, in front of the double-fronted door. Freya froze, paralysed by her fear of dogs. One of her foster parents had had a vicious mutt they'd used to keep the children in order. It had never bitten her, but its ominous snarling and bared teeth had established a terror she'd never got over.

A man shouldered his way through the door. 'Molly, *stay*,' a deep masculine voice commanded.

Ned Hudson. She recognised him immediately as he strode out onto the veranda. Tall, broad-shouldered, more handsome than the photos gave him credit for. He was totally in charge of the dog. At his command, it dropped to the floor. 'Good girl. Miss Delaney is a friend,' he said, as he scratched it behind the ears.

The dog had ceased its fearsome barking but its pink tongue lolled from its scarily sharp white teeth. As long as it didn't come any closer, Freya thought, she'd be okay. She took a deep breath to calm herself. How mortifying to be cringing in terror at a dog on a farm, where, of course, you would expect a dog to be.

'Don't worry about Molly,' Ned Hudson said. 'She's a sweet old girl. Her days working with sheep are over, so she makes it her mission to guard the house. Now I've told her you're a friend she'll drop her guard.'

'Er, that's good,' Freya said, keeping a wary eye on the animal. All dogs, even fluffy little white ones, terrified her. She felt okay with cats but had never owned one. A pet was too much commitment—and commitment scared her more than even the most ferocious dog.

Ned stood at the top of the steps, towering over her, even taller than he looked in the photos, with a strong-jawed face, light brown hair and clear blue eyes. She caught her breath.

Not boring at all.

As he took the steps in just a few long-legged strides she stood transfixed at how attractive she found him. Not her type, of course. But he was so big, so strong, so *rural*. In his dark blue jeans and a blue-and-black checked shirt he was totally in keeping with his surroundings with the confidence of a wealthy man utterly sure of his place in the world.

Whereas she, scared of dogs, with a wide purple stripe in her hair, wearing skinny black jeans, a flowing black top and ankle boots that were perfectly in keeping with her inner-city Melbourne lifestyle, suddenly felt very, very out of place.

All the old insecurities she'd battled so hard to overcome threatened to come rushing back. *She didn't belong here.*

Especially under false pretences—she had no intention of revealing to Ned Hudson that she'd ever known his brother Wil. She would just be Freya the photographer, do her job efficiently and head back down that driveway as soon as she could.

Ned didn't know what he had been expecting the replacement photographer to be like—to be honest he hadn't given her much thought—but Freya Delaney made him look twice. She was about his age, he guessed, petite, slender, arty in the way she dressed and quite lovely—wide cheekbones and a determined jaw saving her from doll-like prettiness. Her pale blonde hair was streaked with purple.

She took a step towards him. 'I'm Freya,' she said. 'Not Miss Delaney. And I'll try not to be too frightened of your dog.'

A slight breeze lifted her long lavender-coloured scarf so it wafted behind her like wings. She laughed as she tried to bat it back into place, twisting and turning as she did so. Her hair shone like a pale gold halo in the morning sun and her eyes gleamed a brilliant shade of blue. Ned wasn't a fanciful man but for a moment she seemed like some fey, other-worldly creature who had flitted in from the rose garden behind her.

He shook his head to clear it of the ridiculous thought.

Where in hell did that come from?

He held out his hand, ready to begin his 'welcome to Five and a Half Mile Creek' spiel but the words choked in his throat and something disconcertingly different came out.

'You like purple,' he said, indicating the purple van, the streak in her hair, the tiny purple stone in her eyebrow ring, more purple glinting at her earlobes.

He knew the comment was inane the second that it slipped out. *Damn.* He could be cursedly awkward when it came to chit-chat. Her eyes widened but she politely shook his hand in a firm grasp for just the required amount of time.

'Yes, I love purple,' she said with a delightful curving of her lips. 'It's the colour of creativity.' Her voice was slightly husky in an intriguing contrast to her very feminine appearance.

'You're a photographer—that makes sense.'

She gave a small, self-deprecating shrug that he found charming. 'Not all my photography is creative,' she said. 'Most of it is commercial, the highlight being a Christmas tree decorated with small cans of cat food instead of baubles.'

He laughed. 'Really? That sounds creative to me.'

Again, that little shrug. 'It did look rather cute. And I believe it sold a lot of cat food. But the shoot was hardly the highlight of my career. I hope wearing purple will better channel my creativity for my own, more artistic photography.'

If anyone else had said that, Ned would have snorted his disbelief. But from this woman it seemed to make a curious kind of sense. She put her left hand to a purple-stoned earring without, he thought, realising she was doing so. He noticed one thing she didn't wear was a purple-stoned ring. Any ring, in fact, on her pale, slender fingers.

'Also my birthday is in February and amethyst is my birthstone.' She paused, flushed high on her cheekbones. 'But you don't want to hear all that.'

But he did. Suddenly Ned wanted to know more about Freya Delaney. 'My mother is very creative,' he said.

'What's her birthstone?' Freya asked.

Now it was his turn to shrug. 'No idea,' he said. It wasn't part of the knowledge bank of a man running thousands of acres devoted to sheep and mixed grains, handling multiple high-stakes investments.

'Your mother is a big name in her field. I looked her up.'

'She's pretty much retired these days.'

Ned was proud of his mother's achievements, the beautiful home she had created for her family on the bones of the historic property. But his mother's creative drive had not come without its demands. Jacqueline Travis had been a city girl at the top of her career game who had fallen for a country guy—and settling down on Five and a Half Mile Creek hadn't been without its problems. Ned knew from painful experience how difficult that had been for her, his father, and him as his mother had battled to both keep up her career and make a home out here. Periodically, she had packed up and headed back to Melbourne for weeks on end—leaving her young son torn between his mother and the home he loved.

Finally, when Ned was nine years old his mother had left his father and wrenched her son away from everything he'd loved to live with her in the city. He could still remember how utterly miserable he'd been away from his pony, his dog, his pet chickens. How impossible it had seemed to have to choose between his mother and his father, both of whom he'd adored.

'According to my boss, Hugh, this house is a wonderful showcase for your mother's talents. It's a shame she can't be here to show me her work.'

'My parents don't live here any more. They moved to Melbourne. But right now they're in Tuscany,' he said.

'Nice,' Freya said with an undertone of longing in her voice.

Ned could have just agreed with her, skated over the truth, but he believed in being straightforward. 'My mother is a breast cancer survivor and—'

Freya gasped and her hand flew to her mouth. 'I'm so sorry,' she said. 'Well, not that she's a survivor but that—'

He had to clear his throat. 'She's been incredibly brave and strong. But she's in remission, thankfully. Now she and my dad are off to see all the places they couldn't see when Five and a Half Mile Creek was their life. No opportunity for extended vacations when you're running a property this size.'

'So now you're in charge.'

'Yes. I took over from my parents so it's all on me now. Not that I'm complaining. I love this place.'

He watched as she looked around her with wide eyes. This was just the house and garden—impressive enough. It was unlikely he'd get the chance to show her there was so much more—the tennis court, swimming pools, an administration office, staff accommodation, historic shearing sheds, horse arena and stables, an airstrip. Thousands of acres of land and the actual creek—really more a small river—from which the property took its name.

'It must be a big job,' she said.

'Yes,' he said. 'But nothing I can't handle.'

The steady hands on the reins.

That was him: steady, reliable, you-can-count-on-me Ned. No one had ever imagined he would say no to the job of running Five and a Half Mile Creek—even if it meant more time spent behind a computer with spreadsheets than on horseback. Ned had known from an early age that his destiny was to run it. There'd been no choice of career for him. He'd excelled at violin but a role in an orchestra had never been an option. Neither had studying to be a veterinarian. When he'd been asked to step up, he'd said *yes*.

He'd only ever strayed from his predestined path once—that crazy time when he'd been so infatuated with Leanne and spent more time in Melbourne with her than he should have. He'd been too blinded by his so-called *love* for her to notice his mother getting frail, his father anxious. His father had actually had to beg him to spend more time at home. When, to Leanne's intense displeasure, Ned had dragged himself unwillingly back from Melbourne, his parents had sat him down and told him about his mother's diagnosis.

Shattered at the news, horrified at his neglect of his duties, he had immediately agreed to move back full-time to Five and a Half Mile Creek while his mother underwent treatment in Melbourne. Foolishly, he'd thought Leanne would come with him, help him heed his wake-up call.

But she hadn't seen his mother's life-threatening cancer as enough reason for her to turn her own life upside down. Certainly not to give him the support he had expected would come freely from the woman he was about to ask to become his wife. He'd never noticed how cold Leanne's eyes could be until she'd told him to hire someone to run his property because she had no intention of leaving Melbourne. He had ended it with her immediately. It had cut deep when he'd realised she wouldn't mourn the loss of him as a boyfriend so much as the lavish expenditure she'd seen as her right.

Ned had regretted that relationship, but had never regretted his decision to do the right thing by his family. Looking back, he wondered whether, when he was a child, his unquestioning acceptance of his destiny was because he had so desperately wanted to please both parents so he could keep them in his life—right here.

But lately he was beginning to feel constricted. Even his wish-list for a wife put Five and a Half Mile Creek's needs first. It wasn't that he wanted to be wild and throw his wonderful life away but sometimes it irked that people seemed to find him so *predictable*. When had he become like that?

'So you took over from your parents,' Freya said. 'Is that why your mother redecorated the house? To mark the new order?'

'It's a family tradition that when the son—and it's always been a son—takes over from the father, he puts his own stamp on the place. My mother met my father when he employed her to redecorate. She came out here and—as Dad says—"captivated" his heart.'

'Aww, that's so romantic,' Freya said with what seemed like genuine appreciation.

'Love at first sight, according to them both.' Another reason for him to avoid relationships based on infatuation.

Head over heels in love.

He'd learned that expression from the story of his parents' 'romantic' meeting. It had never sounded particularly comfortable to him as a child. And it hadn't worked out well for his parents; they'd always seemed to be arguing. He would stick his fingers in his ears so he didn't have to hear their raised, angry voices.

'But it must have been a shock for your mother moving here from Melbourne,' Freya said. 'It's so far away from the city.'

He detected a little shudder of what could be distaste but might have been trepidation. His mother's voice echoed in his ears. *'This place is so far from civilisation.'* It had been a familiar refrain in his earlier years. One he had grown to fear, as it had usually heralded one of his mother's departures.

How he'd hated those times. When he was pre-school age, she had taken him with her. That had meant time spent with her parents, who'd had their grandson in their house under sufferance. He could clearly remember how he'd felt like an unwelcome intruder in their house in the upscale suburb of Kew, stuffed with china ornaments just waiting to be knocked over by a lively little boy. Once he'd started school in Hilltop, the nearest town to Five and a Half Mile Creek, he'd been left with his father when his mother went to work in Melbourne.

While he loved his father, and knew his father loved him, he'd rarely seen him. Running the property was not a nine-to-five job—especially during the years-long drought that had devastated the land. Ned had been placed in the care of a series of nannies ranging from fun and caring, to indifferent, to outright incompetent—none of whom had stayed long. His animals had become his trusted friends and companions. Dogs and horses were so much more reliable than the humans in his life.

But his mother had eventually come to terms with life on the land and his father had learned to delegate and spend more time with his family. When Ned had grown up, his father had tried to explain to him that his enduring deep love for his mother and hers for him was what had driven them to reach the compromise. Ned had felt uncomfortable discussing his parents' love life and had wanted to put his fingers in his ears against that too. More recently his dad had brought the subject up again as the reason why he was handing over the reins—so that two people still very much in love could enjoy every remaining minute of their lives together.

Still, those early painful days when his parents were sorting out their lives were behind much of his criteria for his wife wish-list. Why leave compatibility to chance?

'Without a doubt, it is a long way,' he said. 'You must have left the city very early to get here at this time.' When he visited the city, he cut down the travel time by flying his helicopter or light plane.

She shook her head and her fine hair fell softly around her face. He decided he liked the purple. 'Too far for me to drive all that way in one hit and get here ready to work. I left Melbourne yesterday, then stayed last night at a pub in Hilltop.'

He frowned. 'You should have let me know.

We have a guest cottage. You could have stayed here. It's very comfortable.'

She shook her head rather more fiercely than his question warranted. 'I wouldn't dream of imposing. The pub was fine. I also have my room booked for tonight as this shoot could run to more than one day.'

Ned opened his mouth to say *next time*, before realising there was unlikely to be a next time. Instead he nodded with a non-committal sound.

'I like to work with available light. So I need to get started.' Her voice was brisk and efficient, with that appealing edge of huskiness.

'Do you need a hand with getting equipment in from your van?'

'Thanks, but not yet,' she said. 'I need to assess the shoot first.'

'Then let's get going,' he said. Looking after the photographer had seemed like an intrusion on his busy day, but suddenly it seemed it might become the highlight. He realised that these days he could go weeks without seeing anyone other than the people who worked for him. His regular trips to Melbourne to take in a concert or a band had stopped after the Leanne fiasco.

'The house looks amazing. I can't wait to see inside.' Freya looked up at him and smiled.

He was mesmerised. She had a tiny gap between her two front teeth and it made her smile both quirky and sensual. This close, he noticed her eyes were blue with a darker ring around the edge that was almost purple. His gaze held hers for a moment too long yet he found it impossible to drag his eyes away.

She was beautiful.

But it wasn't just that. He had known Freya for all of ten minutes and yet she seemed somehow familiar, as if there was an inevitability about their meeting. Her smile wavered and she frowned, obviously puzzled.

What the hell?

Did she think he was hitting on her? He dropped his gaze, took a step back.

Freya was here to fulfil an assignment on behalf of her boss. She was an employee of both Hugh Tran and of him on behalf of Five and a Half Mile Creek. And he never, ever showed personal interest in an employee.

His role here was to show her the rooms

she had been engaged to photograph and then leave her to it. It was completely irrelevant whether he found her attractive or not.

More gruffly than he had intended, he asked her to follow him into the house.

CHAPTER TWO

FREYA HAD TO force her gaze away from Ned Hudson's sensational rear view as he strode across the gravel towards the veranda. She didn't want to appreciate the appeal of those broad shoulders, his athletic stride, his impressive butt hugged by blue jeans. Most of all, she didn't want to acknowledge her instant and unsettling attraction to him.

For a long moment just then her eyes had locked with his and she had seen an echo of the same puzzlement she felt at the thought their meeting was somehow...*significant*.

It was a crazy thought and she had to shake herself mentally to get rid of it. For one thing she didn't feel comfortable around this type of man. Ned Hudson was the heir to property and wealth equivalent to a small principality. The 'squattocracy' they called families like the Hudsons, in a play on the word *aristocracy*.

Their ancestors in the early days of the Australian colony had either been granted or had grabbed vast tracts of land—by squatting on it—that they had tenaciously held onto over the years. There wasn't supposed to be a class system in Australia but people like the Hudsons were considered to be blue bloods, as close as Aussies got to landed gentry.

The young men she'd met from that background had been arrogant, with an overblown sense of entitlement. When she was twenty-four, she'd dated one of their kind. She'd thought Henry had been different, and had fallen for him. His snobby mother had openly disapproved of her. But Henry had stood up for her. Until she'd confided in him about her background: daughter of a seventeen-year-old single mum, brought up by her grandparents until they died, then taken into state care at the age of twelve. Everything she had achieved had come from her own hard work and initiative.

Henry had recoiled from her revelation. That she was a photographer made her cool, but her past made her decidedly uncool. He'd stuttered as he'd made it clear that, while what they had together was fun, it was important he marry a woman from the same background as his. She'd walked away, fun over.

Not that Freya ever intended to get married. She refused to give another person—especially a man—power over her life, and certainly not over her heart. She wasn't ashamed of her past; her grandparents had been good people. But the implication that she didn't meet Henry's standards had stung just the same. From then on she'd stuck to dating her own inner-city, creative kind. At least she knew the possible relationship hiccups she faced with those guys. Being not good enough wasn't one of them.

When her boss had entrusted her with this shoot, she'd gone online to research her new client, Ned's mother. If she did the same for Ned, she reckoned she'd find private schooling for him all the way—every privilege inherited money could buy—family trusts and a very easy path in life. He seemed very much a scion of the squattocracy.

Yet her past had taught her not to instantly judge others. After all, Ned's impossibly wealthy family had thrown the door wide open to their privileged life for her old friend Wil, a rebellious, angry teenager. That didn't fit with the behaviour of the so-called elite she had encountered in Melbourne. She would try to keep an open mind.

She followed Ned towards the steps to the veranda, then stopped abruptly as she realised he was leading her towards where the black-and-white border collie sat. Up close, Freya could see her muzzle was silver and one of her eyes cloudy. As she approached, Molly thumped her tail on the wooden floor in greeting. But a dog was a dog and Freya wanted to keep her distance. She couldn't help glancing nervously at the animal—something that didn't escape Ned.

'Molly is more likely to lick you than harm you,' he said. 'Slobbery doggy kisses are her speciality. But I'll put her on her leash, otherwise she'll want to follow you around the house. I'll take her with me when I go back to the office.'

'Thank you,' Freya said on a sigh of relief. 'I know it's ridiculous, but I had a bad experience when I was young and I'm frightened of even small dogs.'

'Not ridiculous at all. But you really have nothing to fear from this old girl.'

He stroked his dog gently around the head with strong, callused hands. How could such a big man be so tender? He looked at Molly with unabashed affection in his eyes and the dog looked adoringly back. How would it feel to have a man look at her like that—open, honest, not afraid to show his feelings? It was something she had never experienced.

'I want to believe you, but I'm happy to keep my distance from her all the same,' she said.

After Ned attached the dog's long leash to a metal ring on the wall, he glanced at his watch. 'I know you're keen to get going so we'd better get you started.'

Freya reached into her tote bag and pulled out a sheaf of printouts. 'Your mother sent a detailed room-by-room shoot list. If you could point me in the direction of the rooms she mentions, I'd appreciate it.' There was no need for him to babysit her.

'Let me have a look,' he said, reaching for the papers and flicking through them. 'Okay, so you need a guide through all this.' He smiled. Again she had to stop herself from staring at him. He had the kind of warm smile that reached his eyes; big, white perfect teeth;

a generous mouth. It was impossible not to respond with a smile of her own.

'Maybe. The house looks enormous and I don't want to get lost or get the rooms wrong.'

'Just follow me,' he said.

Ned pushed open the grand double doors and ushered Freya through ahead of him. With a sense of anticipation, she stepped into a wide corridor, the walls panelled, the wooden floors covered in beautiful, oriental rugs. She paused to glance up at ornately moulded ceilings, and breathe in the scent of beeswax polish and roses from the enormous vase of red blooms on the entry table. As she followed Ned down the corridor, he flung open doors that led into a grand, formal living room with large marble fireplaces and an equally grand dining room.

'This is the more formal part of the house,' Ned explained.

He spoke with a justifiably proprietorial air. What must it be like to have this magnificence as your birthright? It was a far cry from her grandparents' two-bedroom terrace house in the shadow of the brewery where her grandfather had worked for most of his life.

'As a kid I thought it was all stuffy and boring,' he said. 'Now the house is mine, I like those rooms just the way they are.'

'Me too,' she said. Apart from the beauty of the workmanship, the rooms and their furnishings symbolised wealth, continuity, stability—all things she had never experienced.

Ned headed towards the end of the corridor. 'Here's where you'll find the rooms that have had a total makeover. Along here are the family room, the music room, my study, the room that was Mum's studio, and the new kitchen. Mum really went to town to give the house a completely new look for what she calls "the new era of Ned".' He rolled his eyes and Freya smiled.

'You didn't want someone other than your mother to work on the house?'

'She's my mother but she's also Jacqueline Travis, one of Melbourne's top interior designers who loves this house and who knows me very well. Why entrust the design to an outsider? I knew she would do a better job than anyone else.'

'There's that,' Freya said. He must have a good relationship with his parents to be so confident. If so, she envied him. She'd scarcely known her mother, and her father not at all.

He laughed, a deep, full-bodied laugh as engaging as his smile. 'To tell you the truth, I've always been more interested in the outdoors. Refurbishing the stables? I'm your man. I have no interest whatsoever in fabric swatches and colour chips, and the proportions of table lamps. My only stipulation was hard-wearing, comfortable furniture a man could throw himself into without fear of breaking anything.'

Ned was a big man, tall and well built. His shirt sleeves were rolled up to reveal muscular, tanned forearms. His shirt did nothing to disguise a powerful chest. She refused to let her thoughts stray to the rest of his body.

He was a client.

'A wise idea,' she said, suddenly short of breath. Again she had to drag her attention away from him and towards the rooms she had been commissioned to photograph. He was hot, in an understated way that made him seem a degree hotter every time she looked at him. 'Please lead on, you've got me intrigued.'

The first room he showed her was a spacious informal living room. French doors led to the veranda, and a view to pear trees, resplendent in multi-hued autumn leaves. The interior design, while it paid homage to the history of the house, was fresh and contemporary and eminently liveable. Immediately Freya could see angles and details she wanted to capture through the lens of her camera.

Ned gestured to a large, high-backed easy chair covered in a deep blue linen fabric. 'My favourite chair,' he said.

Freya could just imagine him sprawling there, long limbs splayed out, the master of his house. 'It looks strong, yet good-looking too and I suspect it would be very comfortable.' *Like you.*

She bit her lip to stop the words from creeping out unbidden.

What was wrong with her?

Apart from him being a client, this guy was *so* not her type.

'It is,' he said. 'Not that I have an awful lot of time for relaxing. It's a particularly busy time of year with planting and preparations for winter.'

Freya was ignorant of country ways. But this property was vast, and Ned was in charge of it all. She doubted he got down and actually sheared sheep or mended fences. His role would surely be an administrative one. Wasn't a lot of farm routine governed by computers and machines these days?

As he showed her through the rest of the rooms, she checked them against the client's shoot list, getting more and more excited. 'I hope I can do the house justice with my photography.' She had shot some of the finest homes in Melbourne, but to her this was the most beautiful, the most inviting. It was a shame it was a million miles from nowhere.

'I'm sure you will,' he said. 'Hugh Tran wouldn't employ anyone who was anything short of exceptionally talented.'

'That's nice of you to say so.'

'He's a friend of my mother's. I've known your boss all my life.'

'I intend to repay his confidence in me,' she said. 'What about the upstairs? There aren't any bedrooms on the shoot list. Did your mother forget to—?'

'She hasn't touched upstairs.'

Did she not have time to work on those

rooms before she got ill? Freya didn't like to ask. 'Really?' was all she said.

'None of those rooms have had a makeover yet.' He paused, shifted from foot to foot and, for the first time, looked slightly uncomfortable. 'My mother says it's up to my…my… future wife to have the bedrooms the way she wants them.'

'Oh,' Freya said, surprised at the flash of regret she felt. 'You're engaged?'

'No.' He paused. 'But I'll get married some day. Five and a Half Mile Creek needs an heir.'

His offhand comment might have been made as a joke, but it shot her right back to horrible Henry and his talk of marriage as if it were a breeding programme.

'Of course,' she said a little stiffly.

'What about you?' he said.

'Me? Engaged?' She shook her head. 'Nowhere near it.' No need to tell him that she never wanted to get married or why. Or that she hadn't dated for six months. She was here as a photographer, not to swap life stories with the owner of the house.

'How long have you been working for Hugh?' he asked.

'He took me on as his assistant straight out of university. I was lucky to get the chance to work with someone as highly regarded as he is.'

He frowned. 'Surely more than just luck?'

She shook her head. 'Pure luck, really, that I encountered him. When I was a student I was waitressing at a café near his studio. He was a regular.'

She'd put herself through a creative arts degree and had had to scrape for every cent. But she didn't have to share that with Ned. Or further emphasise the differences in their social standing.

'His studio in Richmond?'

'Yes. I had no idea who he was but used to chat with him when I served him his coffee.'

'I bet he had a muffin every day.'

'You know that?'

'My mum and I lived with Hugh and his partner Gordon for a while when I was young and—' Ned stopped abruptly, as if he regretted the words.

'Really?' Freya said, intrigued.

'Long story,' he said, tight-lipped. If she knew Ned better, she might have tried to ca-

KANDY SHEPHERD 47

jole the story out of him. But it wasn't her place to do so.

'Hugh and Gordon are generous and kind,' she said, her voice trailing away, inviting him to say more.

'Yes,' he said, refusing to be led. What *was* that long story about?

Fatherly wasn't quite the word to use about Hugh and the way he'd looked out for her from the get-go. But he was so much more than a boss.

At first she'd been wary of the photographer, as she had tended to be of older guys showing interest in much younger women. But Hugh had proved to be genuine.

'He knew I was a creative arts student—the campus was nearby,' she said. 'But it wasn't until I asked if I could photograph him for an assignment—he has such an interesting face—that I found out who he was and he discovered I was majoring in photography. He posed for me, and the shoot turned out so well I won a university prize for it.'

'Well done,' Ned said.

'Thank you,' she said. 'Hugh was as thrilled as I was.' Once she would have made some

self-deprecating comment about her achieve-
ment. Now she had learned to own her talent
and hard-earned skills.

'Then in my final semester, he let me do a
student placement at his studio. When his assistant left I was beyond delighted when Hugh
offered me the role. I've learned so much from
him. I worked my way up to become a photographer on his team. I couldn't have had a
better mentor.'

'He must have great confidence in you to
have subbed you for this job. I look forward
to seeing the results. Before I go back to work,
I'll introduce you to our housekeeper, Marian. She can answer any further questions you
might have, and give you lunch when you're
ready.'

'No café on the next corner way out here,
when you need a coffee or a snack,' Freya
said—and immediately regretted it. She intended her comment to be light-hearted but it
came out, she feared, more like criticism. 'Not
that I would expect there to be,' she added
hastily. 'There are other wonderful things in
the country besides…er…coffee.'

'Rest assured, we do have coffee in the

house,' he said, rather coldly, she thought. 'Just ask Marian.'

'I…er…will, thank you,' she said.

'Can I help you with your equipment?' Yes, she hadn't imagined it. His tone was cooler, less friendly. It appeared she had unwittingly insulted him. She gave a mental shrug. He was the client. As long as he was polite, he could speak coolly to her. It made no difference.

'Yes. Please.' Not that she couldn't handle all her own gear. But his help getting it into the house would let her get started quicker.

Once her cameras and lenses, tripods, reflectors, diffusers and the laptop she used for work outside the studio were in place, Ned turned to her. 'My mother said for you to help yourself to any flowers from the garden.'

'I brought flowers in buckets from Melbourne for styling purposes. But fresh from the garden would be so much better.' She paused. 'I'd feel a bit nervous about hacking into the plants. I'm not a gardener.'

'Neither am I. But our head gardener is working in the rose garden today. Ask him for whatever you need.'

Gardener. Housekeeper. Freya could only

imagine the number of staff required to keep this gracious house and its grounds looking immaculate. Her grandmother had cleaned houses for the wealthy. 'Thank you for your help,' she said.

He nodded, turned, and left her to it. Suddenly, the room felt very empty.

CHAPTER THREE

NED WAS IN his office in the administration block, which was housed in one of the original structures, built long before the homestead. It had been constructed from stone and timber from the land. His great-grandfather used to refer to it as the 'old house'. Every day, Ned was aware of how much smaller his ancestors must have been, as he had to duck his head to get through the doors.

Today he was preparing for a meeting with the senior members of the farm management team. At this time of year it was vital their efforts were coordinated. But he couldn't settle to his work. His thoughts kept returning to the photo shoot taking place up at the house.

More specifically, his thoughts kept returning to the photographer. Freya. She was smart. Lovely. Intriguing. And a city girl through and through. Scared of dogs. Perhaps equally nervous around horses. Very possibly fearful of lizards and snakes, which, while not often encountered, did share this land with the human occupants.

On his computer, he pulled up the notes from the last meeting, checked the points of action that had been decided. But they were just so many words on the screen. His mind was too occupied by thoughts of the intriguing girl who had appeared so unexpectedly in his life.

He couldn't escape the irony that the first woman he'd found attractive in a long time didn't seem to meet even one of the criteria on his 'wife wish-list'.

Not that it should matter. He certainly wasn't thinking of her as a possible candidate. Their paths wouldn't cross again after the shoot was done. She was a temporary distraction.

But such a lovely distraction.

He glanced at his watch. Usually he would have his lunch delivered from the staff kitchen to his desk. Today he might head up to the house instead. Freya might need some help. Freya might have questions only he could answer. Freya might—

Hell, he just wanted to see Freya.

As Ned approached the kitchen he heard her laughter, and the rise and fall of chatter with his housekeeper, Marian. It was a heart-warming sound he didn't often hear these days. The large house had seemed very empty after his parents had moved away to their new life as 'citizens of Melbourne and the world', as his dad had put it.

Wil's wedding had brought the homestead back to life, packed to the rafters with celebrating family and friends. But a week ago the last guests had packed up and gone home. Now, in the evenings, the sound of his lone footsteps on the wooden floors echoed through the rooms. Some nights the only voice he heard was his own, talking to his faithful dog, Molly, who did her best to talk back. Not that he felt sorry for himself. He was used to his own company and, during the day, he interacted with the staff. It was his home that felt empty. Freya's laughter brought it to life.

He paused just outside the threshold to the kitchen. Freya sat at the table in the generous eat-in area that led off the cooking area. A steaming bowl of soup sat in front of her. Pumpkin and lentil by the smell of it, a favourite of his. She looked very comfortable, her face animated, as if she belonged there. But as he walked into the room, the chatter stopped abruptly.

Her eyes widened with dismay as she caught sight of him. 'Just having a quick lunch break,' she said, as if she'd been caught out neglecting her work. She pushed back her chair and made to get up.

Was he so formidable? His favourite cousin, Erin—she of the *'never a groom'* prediction at the wedding—had told him he needed to lighten up, that he had what she called a 'resting stern face'. He gestured for Freya to sit down. 'Don't get up. Please. Enjoy your lunch.' He reckoned a forced smile was perhaps worse than stern, so he didn't attempt one.

Freya sat back into her chair, picked up her spoon, then put it back down again. She pushed the bowl away from her. 'Actually, I must be getting back to work.'

Just when he'd joined her? Ned was surprised at how disappointed he felt. He frowned. 'Not right now, surely?' If that could be seen as pulling rank, he didn't care. Of course he had come up to the house just to see her; he couldn't deny that to himself any longer.

'I…er…do have a lot more to get done,' she said.

'Do you want lunch here, Ned?' Marian asked. 'Rather than in your office?' Marian ran the household efficiently and pleasantly. She'd proved to be a gem when his mother had fallen ill. Now she was invaluable to him in all matters household.

'Now that I'm here, lunch sounds like a good idea,' he said, as he pulled out the chair opposite Freya. Her hair with its cute purple stripe was pulled right back from her face, highlighting the slant of her cheekbones, her lush mouth. She'd ditched her scarf and shapeless long tunic for a black T-shirt that revealed subtle, yet pleasingly shapely, curves. 'How is your photography going?'

'Wonderful. Your house is a dream to shoot. When you've finished your lunch, why don't you come find me and I can show you some of the frames?'

She didn't meet his eye and he wondered why she seemed nervous when she certainly hadn't at their previous meeting.

'I'll do that,' he said.

'Ned, I…' She stopped.

'Yes?'

She leaned towards him, lowered her voice. 'I feel bad about my café remark earlier. You know, implying that you're too far from civilisation out here to have decent coffee. I didn't mean to offend but I fear I did.'

Too far from civilisation. Ned froze momentarily at her use of that phrase—so similar to his mother's words that had wreaked such havoc in his young life. But he quickly recovered. 'No offence taken,' he said gruffly.

'Thank you.' She smiled that appealing gap-toothed smile with obvious relief. 'First rule of commercial photography—never insult the client.'

'I wasn't insulted,' he said with a slow grin. 'It wasn't the first time I've heard a comment like that, believe me.' Not insulted, but disappointed when she had come out with the clichéd criticism.

'Just the same, it was wrong of me to pass judgement on a way of life that I know nothing about. And then of course I discover that

Marian worked as a barista in Sydney and you have coffee here as good as any inner-city café. Fabulous food too. It's humble pie I should be eating, not soup.'

'Thank you, Freya, all compliments gratefully accepted,' Marian called over her shoulder from where she stood at the stove. Ned was surprised at the warmth in the usually reserved, middle-aged housekeeper's voice.

'We lead a very good life here,' he said. 'I would never swap country life for the city. Crowds and cars and endless rush are not for me. Not any more.' He wished he could show Freya the slow pleasures of rural life but he suspected she was on a city timetable where every moment counted in the rush to the next thing.

'Each to his own,' Freya said lightly. 'I'm a city person myself, bright lights and action, but I can appreciate the appeal of the country.'

She got up from her chair. 'I'm shooting in your study,' she said. 'Will I see you there?'

'Give me ten minutes,' he said.

When Ned got to the study, it was to find Freya intent on her work. She was bent from the waist, huddled low over her camera, which was set on a tripod with a twist of cables falling from it. The angle of her body was a perfect showcase for her pert behind and slender legs clad in skinny black jeans. Her T-shirt had ridden up to reveal an enticing glimpse of pale skin. He tried very hard not to stare.

'You're here,' she said, without looking back or taking her eye from the viewfinder. 'What a wonderful room. The gentleman's study updated.'

'It was my father's and my grandfather's before that. My father wanted the room kept the way his father had it, dark furniture, leather and smelling of old cigarette smoke.'

'It certainly doesn't look like that now,' she said.

His mother had completely transformed the room, ripping up the carpet, throwing out the velvet curtains, furnishing the room simply in neutral colours. His office in the administration block was for work; this was his private domain for his books, his personal computer, the horse paintings he had been given as gifts over the years. Now that it was more to his taste, he considered it a haven.

'I still haven't got used to this room being mine,' he said. 'I thought it would be many years before I took it over.'

'You're a lucky man to have grown up here,' she said briefly.

He couldn't debate that.

Her camera seemed to be trained on a disparate collection of items on a corner of his desk. There was an old book with a fraying fabric cover—an early history of Five and a Half Mile Creek; an expensive fountain pen he had been given for his twenty-first birthday but had never used; and a lucky horseshoe from Banjo, his first pony, propped against the book. Ned had nothing to hide, but he found it disconcerting that Freya had looked through the desk drawer and the bookshelves to find them—even though he had told her to help herself to anything she needed. He valued his privacy.

'The horseshoe,' he said. 'You've got it placed the wrong way.'

'Does it matter?' He could hear the frown in her voice.

'You're meant to have it open end up, so it collects good luck in the curve,' he said. 'If you have it the other way, the luck drains away.'

She glanced up at him. 'Do you seriously believe that? I wouldn't have taken you for the superstitious type.'

'I've had that horseshoe since I was a kid. It's always been displayed open end up,' he said stubbornly.

'Move it for me, then,' she said, returning to her viewfinder. 'But please be careful not to disturb anything else. I'm happy with this composition.'

Ned stepped in front of the camera and carefully turned the horseshoe around so it sat the correct way. He started at the sudden burst of the camera's motor drive and glared at her accusingly. 'Did you just photograph me?'

'Couldn't resist the image of your hand with the horseshoe,' she said without looking up. 'I think it could be cute.'

Cute? It wasn't a word that was ever used to describe him. 'Okay,' he said, bemused.

'Now hop out of the way, will you, please? I've been waiting for the sun to move out from behind a cloud to get the perfect light. Here it comes—' She paused. 'Darn. Not quick enough. You distracted me.'

Ned wasn't used to being ordered around by an attractive woman the same age as him. It was quite a novelty. Of course, he could remind her of who was the boss around here. But he admired her professionalism, her total focus on her work, her straightforwardness. He liked her honesty too. Honesty was important to him.

'We had to get that horseshoe right,' he said.

We. He hadn't meant to say *we.* This wasn't teamwork. She was here to do a job. He was here to facilitate her work. That was all.

'If you say so. I know nothing about horses or horseshoes.' She stilled. 'Wait. The light's perfect.' Again the sound of the motor drive.

'You got it?'

'Yep.' Freya stood up, flexing her back in a graceful, highly sensuous motion that fascinated him. Maybe she did yoga or dance. 'Do you want to look through the lens?' she asked.

He had to clear his throat. 'Why not?'

'You're the boss. If you're unhappy with the image, I'll try again.'

Freya stayed disconcertingly close as she showed him where to look on the camera. He was aware of her scent—something fresh and feminine, that brought to mind the flower garden he'd imagined she'd wafted in from. Right now, without her floaty scarf and dressed all in black, she seemed less ephemeral and very much more grounded and practical.

He looked through the lens—and was taken aback by her talent. This image was not a mere cataloguing of his mother's skills. It was a work of art. The book and horseshoe display on his desk was part of a broader image that expertly showcased the clever redesign of the room. The French doors opened to the garden, revealing a blur of autumn colour from the garden like a painted backdrop to the room. Somehow she'd included, on the nearest wall, the pen-and-wash painting of his favourite polo pony, Hero, that Wil had commissioned for him as a gift for being his best man.

He pulled away from the viewfinder and stood back up. 'How did you do that? Was it a special lens?'

'That would be giving away trade secrets,' she said archly, but looked pleased.

'It's brilliant,' he said. 'You've captured the design of the room but also the—'

'The heart,' she said. 'I could see you wondered why on earth I would choose to show the old book, the pen, the horseshoe.'

'How could you tell that?'

She laughed. 'You have an open face. Your feelings are no secret.'

How many times had he felt disconcerted in the short time he'd known her? 'Well, I—'

'I see your openness as a good thing. Better than the opposite, being cagey and closed off.' Her expression tightened momentarily and he wondered about her past. All he knew about her was her work history with Hugh, which, he reminded himself, was all he needed to know.

'Uh, that's good,' he said. So, did he have an open, revealing face or a 'resting stern face'? The way women put things sometimes baffled him.

'I try to bring the essence of the person into the room, hence the personal items,' she explained. 'In this case, the old book and the old-fashioned fountain pen represent the owner's heritage, the computer his modern-day reality. The horseshoe and the painting of the magnificent horse reveal something of his, er… your, interests.'

'Without giving away too much of the man,' he said thoughtfully.

'Would you like to see some of the morning's shoot?'

'I'd like that very much,' he said, suddenly very curious. What Freya mightn't realise was that her choice of objects and angles revealed something about herself too. Thoughtful, looking beyond the obvious, intuitive.

She picked up the laptop that sat on a low table nearby. 'Keep in mind these images are raw. I'll process and edit them when I get back to the studio. I bracket the shot, using different camera settings. But the folder I'll take you through has what I think might be the winners.'

Ned watched as she flashed through her morning's work on screen. Her style soon became apparent. There was something intimate in each image that brought a person's presence into the room and made it so much more than a cataloguing of furnishings and finishes. He had to laugh at her shot of his old work boots on the edge of the veranda. Who would have thought they would be worthy of artistic interpretation? 'I'm seeing the house where I grew up in quite a different way,' he marvelled.

'Of course you are. I'm seeing what is familiar to you for the very first time. Free of any memories. I'm hardly going to see it the same way you do.'

'But what you choose to emphasise, the angles you work with, are so unexpected.'

'Just my interpretation,' she said with that cute shrug.

'Your artist's eye?'

'If you like. Although these rooms are so wonderfully designed I reckon you could blindfold me, spin me around, let me randomly shoot and you'd still get a good picture.'

'I don't believe that for a moment. You're highly skilled. No wonder Hugh took you on straight from uni.' He narrowed his eyes as he looked again at the images on the screen. 'You've shown me possibilities I never thought about, made me question the familiar.'

'It's what I do,' she said simply. 'I suspect it's what all artists aim to achieve.'

'You've succeeded on every level.'

She flushed high on her cheekbones. 'Thank you. I love shooting interiors. Although I shoot food too. Some fashion and beauty. I'm an all-rounder.'

'Cat-food cans on Christmas trees?'

She laughed. 'That too. But interiors are my special interest, especially non-commercial. That's why Hugh thought I'd enjoy this assignment.'

Ned turned to look down at her. Her face was flushed and strands of her hair had escaped her hair tie and were wisping around her face. Some of them were purple. He resisted the urge to reach out and brush them back from her face. Her skin would be smooth and warm beneath his fingers. 'Are you enjoying it?'

She looked up at him, her brow pleated into a light frown. 'I am. Actually even more than I thought I would. There's something special about this place. I wasn't expecting…' Her voice trailed away.

There's something special about *you*. Again Ned had that sensation that Freya's presence here was meant to be. He found it deeply unsettling. Did that show on his supposedly easy-to-read face? He stepped right back from her. 'I'm glad to hear that.'

She closed the on-screen folder with the images he had been admiring. He noticed her hand wasn't quite steady.

'I even enjoyed the garden. I told you I'm not a gardener. And I know photographing the garden wasn't part of the brief.' She was speaking too quickly, avoiding his gaze.

Did she feel it too?

'But when your gardener was cutting me some roses, I took the opportunity to take a few shots.'

'I'd like to see them,' he said.

'Okay,' she said, opening another folder on her laptop. 'There's just a few, I only had ten minutes.' She scrolled through close-up images of roses, a black-and-white Australian magpie against autumn foliage, a bee burrowing into purple lavender flowers.

'These are magnificent. I reckon you've got a future in garden photography too.'

'Not all gardens are as spectacular as these,' she said.

'My mother will be thrilled. These are an unexpected bonus.'

Freya glanced down at her watch. 'She won't be thrilled if I don't get through her shoot list. I need to get on with it if I'm to finish before the light fades too much. I'll be done then and can head back to Melbourne this afternoon.'

'This afternoon?' He forced the shock from his voice. 'I thought you said you'd need two days to finish the shoot?'

'That was when I thought I'd be shooting bedrooms too. It turned out to be a smaller gig.'

She would be gone by the evening. He wouldn't see her again. Perhaps *ever*.

He couldn't let that happen.

'When you've finished and we still have light, why don't I take you up in my helicopter so you can see the rest of the property?'

Her eyes widened. 'I'd like that.'

He flew his own helicopter?

Ned continued to surprise Freya—not so much by his skills but by how much she enjoyed his company. She couldn't remember when she'd last chatted so easily with a good-looking man. His quiet steadiness made her feel at ease.

She liked him.

There were things she was curious about, like why this big, tough country guy was superstitious about horseshoes. And why he wasn't already married and filling this vast, empty house with 'heirs'. They tended to marry young in the country, didn't they? What else was there to do?

If Ned didn't live way out here at the back of beyond, and she in inner-city Melbourne, she might suggest they caught up for a drink some time. She could see herself being friends with him.

Just friends.

Okay, maybe more than friends. She couldn't deny she found him incredibly attractive. But that wasn't going to happen. There was a truckload of reasons why that couldn't happen. Still, she felt sad she would be saying goodbye to him in just a few hours.

Ned left her to go back to his work and she to hers. She watched him as he strode away, again admiring his back view and the confidence and strength that seemed innate in him.

Again the room seemed preternaturally empty when he'd gone, as if he took the energy—the *essence*—of the space with him. She shook her head to clear her mind. It was weird to have these thoughts about a man she'd only known a few hours.

Excited at the prospect of a helicopter ride, she pushed through the rest of her work so the shoot list would be complete while the light was still good.

Freya had never ridden in a helicopter before and the experience was exhilarating. Ned sat in the pilot's seat in front and she beside him. They were strapped in by harness-style seat belts and wore large, noise-cancelling head-phones to protect against the noise of the rotor blades and engine. They had to use micro-phones for communication. Any nervousness she'd felt dissipated as she saw how skilfully and confidently he controlled the helicopter. He was a man born to be in charge.

'We mainly use the helicopter to muster sheep,' Ned explained. 'Although I still pre-fer mustering on horseback the old-fashioned way. But it's a nice way to introduce you to the property.'

Freya was clueless about farming. But she was enthralled by the close three-hundred-and-sixty-degree views of the extensive lands belonging to Five and a Half Mile Creek. Below was a patchwork of extensive ploughed fields of rich, fertile soil, some a haze of luminous green with what Ned explained was newly planted winter crops of wheat and barley.

In the fading light of the afternoon, long shadows fell from the surrounding hills and gave the landscape a surreal quality. It was almost beyond her comprehension that one man could own so much land. And that they hadn't even reached its borders.

'This is a whole new world to me,' she said, snapping off some images on her smartphone through the clear windows. 'It's awe-inspiring.'

Vast tracts of fenced land were home to slow-moving mobs of sheep heading for stands of eucalypt trees, and dams. Throughout the property ran the snaking lines of the creek—a river to her eyes—that gave the property its name, with eucalypts growing along its banks.

Ned swooped down to show her flocks of wild ducks on the surface of the water, so close the grass flattened and the water rippled.

He took her on an eagle's-eye-view tour of the homestead and gardens, then showed her what lay beyond the boundaries of the garden: the art-deco-style building that housed an indoor heated swimming pool; the blue rectangle of an outdoor pool; a full-sized tennis court. Ned explained he didn't swoop too low across the stable complex and training arenas because he didn't want to spook the horses grazing in the surrounding lush green paddocks. The staff accommodation seemed like a small village. Freya was stunned at the size and complexity of the place—it was impossible to imagine what it must be like to live here, to have grown up here, the sense of privilege and entitlement that must come with being born to such a place.

She didn't want the ride to end, but the light started to fade and Ned told her it was time to head for home. She felt a surprising level of disappointment as they dropped down to earth from her sojourn in the sky.

Once the rotor blades stilled and the engine

noise abated, she took off her headphones and turned to Ned. 'Thank you for that, I'll never forget it.'

'I could tell how much you enjoyed the tour. I never take this place for granted but it was good to see the land afresh through your eyes, the same as you showed me a different aspect of my home through the lens of your camera.'

He told her one of the men would drive her back up to the house and he would see her before she left.

By the time she'd finished packing up her equipment, darkness had fallen and Freya felt overwhelmed by a nagging sense of melancholy. She didn't expect that Ned would come back to the house. Why should he? He'd taken time out from his work to give her the helicopter tour. He had already approved the early images on his mother's behalf. There was nothing further he needed to say to her. But she felt the need to say goodbye, to see him one more time.

She had thanked Marian for her help and was loading her gear into her van, saying a mental farewell to Five and a Half Mile Creek, when its boss was suddenly there, looming up next to her in the shadows. Her heart started a furious, irrational pounding.

'You're going?' he said.

'Yes,' she said, fighting to keep her voice even.

'I put the helicopter to bed but then got caught up in something else.'

'I didn't expect—'

'It's a long way to drive on your own.'

'I'll check into a motel on the way to break the journey.'

'How busy are you next week?' Was *he* going to suggest they catch up?

'Not too busy. It depends what Hugh has booked for me. Why?' She held her breath for his answer.

'I'd like you to come back and photograph the garden. Not for me. For my mother. As a surprise. For her birthday in June. Each milestone for her is precious and she would love—'

'Yes,' Freya said.

'Yes?'

She nodded. 'Yes. I'll do it.'

'Could you do Monday or Tuesday? The autumn garden is at its best now, the weather could turn at any time and—'

'I can do it either day.'

'You don't have to check your planner?'

'No. Those days are free.' If they weren't, she would make sure they were free. Even if she had to postpone jobs. Even if Hugh wasn't happy about it.

'You can stay here at the guest cottage.'

'That won't be necessary. I—'

'I insist.'

She shrugged, both defeated and elated at the same time. 'The cottage it is,' she said. 'How about I drive up Sunday so I can start Monday?'

'You might need to work Tuesday too. It's a big garden.'

'Agreed,' she said.

'You'll stay at the guest cottage Sunday and Monday nights.'

She hesitated, then put out her hand for him to shake. 'It's a deal,' she said.

He grasped her hand in his own much larger one in a firm, hard grip. Her hand seemed to tingle at his warmth and strength. Again came that curious feeling that it was more than seal-ing an agreement for a photographic shoot.

'A deal,' he said, in that gruff, deep voice.

She paused. 'June. That's pearl.'

His dark brows drew together in a quizzical expression. 'And that means...?'

'Pearl is your mother's birthstone, if her birthday is in June.'

He laughed. 'So now I know. It's taken me nearly thirty years, but now I know.'

She laughed too as she withdrew her hand, said goodbye, and drove away, still with a smile curving her mouth.

She felt irrationally pleased that she would be returning to Five and a Half Mile Creek. Also very aware that if she did so, she would have to confess to Ned that she knew Wil and that the story of her life would have to unravel along with that confession.

CHAPTER FOUR

FREYA'S RETURN TO Five and a Half Mile Creek five days later was very different from her first visit. Ned was there on the veranda waiting for her. Just Ned, with no scary dog in tow. Big, tall, gorgeous Ned who had been on her mind way too much back home in Melbourne. He waved, a broad sweep of his arm that said *welcome*. His smile was warm, genuine and aimed at her with what seemed like real pleasure. His hotness factor soared a few degrees higher. Even though he was still definitely not her type.

When she stepped out of her van it seemed natural for him to sweep her into a hug and for her to fall willingly into it. A *friendly* hug. She wasn't reading any more into it than that.

But it felt so good she had to close her eyes to try and gather her rioting senses. His chest was a wall of solid muscle, his arms firm and powerful around her. Held so close, she was intensely aware of Ned as a man. His warmth, his strength, his spicy male scent—with an undertone of what she suspected might be hay. Being in his arms was exciting. And something else—something unaccustomed—she couldn't quite put a name to. *Safe.* That was what it was. And feeling safe with a man scared the hell out of her.

She pulled away from the hug, made a play of patting her hair into place and picking up her small overnight bag from the front seat.

'Let me take that,' Ned said, reaching for the bag. 'The cottage is ready for you.'

She hesitated. 'My gear. It needs to come in.'

'You can leave it in your van.'

'I never leave my stuff in the van.'

Ned laughed. 'You're not parked on a Melbourne street. Your equipment will be perfectly safe. You can even leave the van unlocked.'

She frowned. 'I guess there's no one nearby to steal anything.' Had she inadvertently insulted him again? On the long drive from Melbourne, she had been reminded of how very far away Five and a Half Mile Creek was from the city. When she'd been up in the helicopter with Ned they hadn't seen any other dwelling, his land stretched so far.

'Correct,' Ned said, not sounding in the least bit insulted.

'If you're sure,' she said, unable to stop the doubtful note from entering her voice. She lived in a densely populated urban area where no one left anything of value in their cars.

'I guarantee everything will still be there in the morning,' he said. 'But if it makes you happy, we can take it into the cottage.'

She took a deep breath. Put her hand up in a halt sign. 'No. I'll take your word for it. I... I trust you.' *Trust.* That wasn't something she was used to when it came to men.

'I'm glad to hear that,' he said with that slow smile she was beginning to find so appealing. 'You really can trust me, you know.' His gaze held hers for a long moment until she looked away, flustered. Did he mean something more than the obvious?

'I'll bring my cameras and lenses and of course my laptop.' She spoke too quickly. 'The rest can stay out here. But I will lock the van. And activate the alarm.'

'Whatever makes you feel secure,' he said.

Him.

Ned.

Freya had a from-out-of-nowhere feeling *he* could make her secure. Which was crazy considering their differences. And her fierce determination to maintain her independence. She didn't need to be looked after.

'Now give me that bag and we'll get you to the cottage. It's not far from the house, just down this pathway.'

Freya fell in step beside him. She was wearing flat boots and had to look a long way up to him. For every broad stride he took, she had to take two steps to keep up. 'I feel like I'm being meet-and-greeted at a posh country-house hotel,' she commented.

Uncanny how she felt immediately at ease with him again, as if there hadn't been nearly a week since she'd last seen him.

'The cottage is comfortable. But perhaps not posh hotel standard,' he said. She could hear the smile in his voice.

'Oh, but it is,' she exclaimed when Ned ushered her into the cottage. 'It's beautiful. Like a suite in the poshest of country-house retreats. But then what else would I expect in this place?'

Ned told her the guest cottage had been built some time in the nineteen seventies, to echo the Victorian style of the main house. But inside it had been completely updated—by his mother no doubt; Freya was beginning to recognise her signature style. The cottage was light and spacious with a roomy living area, two bedrooms, two bathrooms, a full-sized kitchen and a utility room. It would contain her tiny apartment in the inner eastern Melbourne suburb of Richmond several times over.

If she had it in her to be envious, Freya would envy Ned the wonderful place he lived in, where even a guest cottage was worthy of a lifestyle shoot. There was also the enviable security of growing up in a happy family environment with a securely married mother and father. What seemed to her a dream childhood was worth even more than the obvious wealth he had been born into. Instead of envy she was happy for him, and more than happy the magic circle had been extended to include Wil.

Wil. She would have to bring up her connection to his brother sooner rather than later. Otherwise her omission would always be hanging over any interaction with Ned.

Ned carried her bag into the largest room. 'I think you'll be comfortable in here.'

'How could I not be comfortable in such a fabulous place?' she said.

Freya followed him in, which led them to both standing next to a large queen-sized bed. She and Ned so close to a *bed*.

It conjured up a sudden image of such over-whelming sensuality, of them together on that bed, that she could feel her cheeks begin to colour. She didn't dare look at the bed—or at Ned. Rather she turned away and admired the view from the French doors, which opened out into a private courtyard. A stream of nervous exclamations escaped her. There was a bird-bath! And look at that lovely carved garden bench! Oh, and a climbing rose!

When her chatter petered out, she noticed Ned looked as awkward as she felt. He shifted from foot to foot. His gaze was averted from the bed too. 'I'll leave you to it,' he said. 'I hope you'll join me for dinner up at the house.'

'Thank you,' she managed to choke out.

Ned went to leave the room, hesitated, and then turned back. 'I look forward to seeing you later.' He dipped his head as he spoke and, to her astonishment, Freya realised this boldly confident man was shy. More to the point, shy around *her*.

She already liked Ned. This revelation only served to further endear him to her. 'I'm looking forward to seeing you too,' she said softly, looking up into his eyes. Still shocked by that erotic image of the two of them together on the bed, she fought the compulsion to reach up and kiss him on the cheek. Not a good idea. She was beginning to wonder what a simple touch might ignite.

But after he left, she sat hunched over on the edge of the bed and rested her face in her hands. What would Ned think of her when he discovered who she was? While she hadn't out-and-out lied to him, her silence when it came to the fact she had known his brother Wil would seem like a blatant act of dishonesty. And she had a very strong feeling Ned would not react well to that.

She wouldn't unpack her bag. There seemed little point as there was a real risk that when she confessed who she was, the truth about her background, Ned would react like everyone else in his social strata—with distaste at her humble origins. He could very well cancel the garden assignment and she'd be back on the road to Melbourne tonight. Lucky she'd left her photographic gear in the van.

But there was still the meal with him to face, so she had to shower and get ready. Would she be expected to dress for dinner? On the off chance, she'd packed a simple black jersey dress that fell to just above the knee and had three-quarter sleeves and a scoop neck. She could dress it up with her favourite lavender scarf around her shoulders against the cool of the April evening and her amethyst pendant, the only thing that she had from her beloved grandmother. She brushed her hair around her shoulders and applied more make-up than she usually wore. For some inexplicable reason, she couldn't escape the feeling she was going in to battle for something very important.

When Ned was on his own for dinner—which was more often than not the case these days— he ate in the informal dining area that led off the kitchen, with Molly by his side. But that felt too casual, too domestic, for a dinner with the boss of Five and a Half Mile Creek and the visiting photographer.

Instead, he'd elected to have dinner in the formal dining room. He thought Freya might appreciate the beautiful, nineteenth-century mahogany furniture imported from England so long ago by his ancestors, the priceless Persian carpets, the ornate chandeliers. The table sat twelve, and at one end places for two had been set with polished silver, gold-edged china and crystal stemware. Roses from the garden sent a heady scent through the room.

Marian had prepared the food, to be served by one of the young household staff. A simple meal, served spectacularly, his housekeeper had said.

Ned stood up to greet Freya as Marian ushered her into the dining room. *'Wow,'* she said, looking around her. 'When you said dinner, you really meant dinner party. This is fabulous. I feel I should be wearing a ball gown.'

Wow, Ned thought about Freya, who looked every bit as elegant as if she were in formal dress. She wore her purple wings—uh, gauzy scarf—which she slipped off to drape across the back of her chair. Her black dress, while not provocatively sexy, clung enticingly to her curves. The neckline revealed a tantalising hint of cleavage. Her pale hair tumbled below her shoulders and her mouth was slicked with glossy pink lipstick.

'You look very nice the way you are,' he said.

Nice was a safe, unloaded word she couldn't read anything more into. He swallowed a curse word when he remembered his reaction to being alone with her in the cottage.

Him. Her. A bedroom.

He'd had to curl his hands into fists to stop himself from reaching out for her and kissing her, from fantasising about sweeping her into his arms and carrying her to the bed. His wildly erotic thoughts were inappropriate, unwarranted, completely out of order as she was, if not an employee, a contractor. But he couldn't deny it. She was gorgeous.

And he wanted her.

Even if he couldn't do anything about it.

He offered her a flute of vintage champagne he'd brought up from the cellar. 'To celebrate a photographic shoot well done—my mother was delighted with the results,' he said.

'I wish all my clients celebrated in such style,' she said, raising the flute to her lips, looking over the rim up at him.

'You delivered superlative work,' he said.

'Thank you. I hope to do as well for you with the garden shoot.'

'I don't doubt for a minute that you will,' he said.

She looked around her, fixing her gaze on a portrait of his great-great-great-grandfather. 'Does this very grand room get used often?'

'Surprisingly, yes. My mother used to say there was no point in having all this if we didn't enjoy it. We often had family meals here and entertained too. Dad reckoned it was a good way for me to learn table manners and how to behave in company. I learned the correct knife and fork to use but some of those long dinners could be interminably boring to a young boy. I can still remember looking out of the window and aching to be outside.'

'It all looks very…civilised,' she said. A smile hovered at the corners of her mouth.

'So you concede a further touch of civilisation to this place?'

'I have no other choice,' she said. 'This room and all that's in it must have been the height of culture in its time.'

'Absolutely. The house wasn't built just for the family's comfort but also as a display of wealth and prosperity. In the old days, visitors from the city or other far-flung properties would stay a few days. Prime ministers and other notables dined here and stayed the night on tours of the district.'

'It's so different from the way I live, I find that difficult to relate to. It's like a parallel universe.'

'It's my world,' he said. 'But that's not to say I haven't enjoyed my times in the city too. My family has a house in Toorak and a few years back I bought an apartment not far from them. It's rarely used now though.'

'That's a shame,' she said.

Ned shrugged. 'It's there for when I need it.' He certainly wasn't going to share the Leanne fiasco with Freya. He'd spent so much time with her there he found it difficult to revisit—not because he missed her but because he didn't want to be reminded about what a fool he'd been to be taken in by her.

'Melbourne is such a great place to live,' she said.

'Tell me why you love it so much,' he said.

She smiled. 'Do we have all night?'

'How about your top five reasons?'

'Only five? Let me think.' She paused, put her hand under her chin in exaggerated thinking mode. 'Do you really want to hear this?'

'Yes,' he said.

'I guess the general buzz of the city, people everywhere, life, action, the river, there's always something to do. Melbourne is cultural, hip. I love the laneway cafés, the bars, the restaurants, the markets, the buskers. Last week there was a girl sitting on a milk crate on the footpath with an old-fashioned typewriter and she wrote me a poem; in return I took an arty photo of her in black and white and emailed it to her. It's fun to take high tea in one of the posh hotels. The shops, of course, the fabulous shops.' She smiled. 'I should stop now, but there's more.'

'Keep going,' he said.

'Okay. Then there are the museums, the art

galleries, the concerts, the art-house movies, even the graffiti. Oh, and the exhibitions. The world comes to Melbourne with exhibitions from archaeological to pop culture to the costumes worn in the greatest movies.' Her face was animated, her cheeks flushed, eyes shining. 'I go to see them all.'

'I used to like the music, pub bands, concerts, jazz clubs, the buskers and sidewalk theatre,' he said.

'Those too,' she said.

'I busked myself once, down by Flinders Street Railway Station, when I was a uni student. I was embarrassed when people actually threw money in my violin case.' He'd tipped his earnings into the hat of a fellow busker who'd looked as if he needed the money.

'Seriously? You must be very good.'

'Out of practice now,' he said dismissively. He'd blocked from his mind how much, at one time, he'd enjoyed life in Melbourne. But he'd been needed at home.

She laughed. 'I've gone way over the five-reason limit on why I love city life, haven't I?'

'I'm sure there are more,' he said.

'Actually...' She drew the word out and

laughed. 'I'll spare you my further reasons. But, seriously, you have a place in Melbourne and never use it?'

'I do if I need to visit the city. Otherwise my brother Wil stays there when he's in Melbourne on business so it's not totally neglected.'

'Th-that's good,' she said.

Freya suddenly quietened. All that animation and vivacity switched off. Ned racked his brains to think if he had said anything untoward but he didn't get a chance to follow it up as their first course arrived—a salad of figs and pecans, both grown in their orchard, with leaves from the kitchen garden.

He wondered why Freya suddenly seemed to find it so difficult to relax. Was the setting for dinner too formal for her? By the time the Italian-style chicken dish was served, conversation between them had dwindled.

The only time Freya seemed really engaged was when they discussed the garden shoot for the following day. She wasn't eating much, pushing her food around her plate with her fork. The white wine in her glass remained untouched.

Ned found the stilted conversation increasingly uncomfortable. 'Are you okay?' he said finally. 'Are you concerned about the shoot?'

Freya put her fork down and looked him straight in the eye. She took a deep breath, which caused a delightful swelling of her breasts above her neckline, then took another as if she was girding herself.

'Ned,' she said. 'I can't put it off any longer. I... I have to tell you something. Something about myself.'

'Okay,' he said slowly, taken aback.

'I... I haven't been completely honest with you...'

There was something about her expression that made him believe he wasn't going to like what she said. She was married. She was engaged. She wasn't interested in men. Those were his main concerns. Oddly, if she confessed to having a criminal record he mightn't care so much. Her single status was more important. Which was insane, when she didn't check one box on his wife wish-list.

'Really?' he said, his voice thick with dread of what he might hear.

'I… I…' She groaned. 'I don't know where to start.'

'Is it that complex?'

'Yes, it is.' Her face contorted with anxiety and what might be poorly masked fear.

Fear of him?

Perhaps it was his 'resting stern face'. Ned forced himself to look calm, receptive, even though his thoughts were churning. 'Why don't you start with the most important thing you think I need to know?'

She chewed at her bottom lip, pulled at her lock of purple hair without, he thought, seeming to realise it. Then took another deep breath, exhaled it on a sigh. 'Ned… I… I'm not who I say I am. At least I wasn't when—'

'What do you mean?'

Her mouth turned down. 'My name is Freya, but I… I went by another name when I knew your brother Wil.'

'You know Wil?' The words exploded from him.

'Yes.'

A sickening disappointment churned through him. Wil was a very handsome guy who effortlessly attracted women. Ned loved him, was incredibly grateful he had him as a brother, but it wouldn't be the first time some girl had wheedled her way into friendship with him in an effort to get to his charismatic younger brother.

'You're one of his ex-girlfriends? He's married now. You need to leave him alone.'

His words were purposefully harsh. Wil was happy with Georgia; he deserved that happiness. Ned couldn't condone an obsessed former girlfriend showing up here at Five and a Half Mile Creek misrepresenting herself and trying to cause trouble. To think he'd found himself fantasising about Freya. One of his brother's cast-offs. The thought brought a nasty taste to his mouth.

He'd got her so wrong.

Freya shook her head. 'No! Ned. It's not like that at all. I'm not an ex-girlfriend. I'm so glad Wil has found a wonderful wife. You can't imagine how happy that makes me feel. I—'

He was not inclined to believe her. 'Then who are you?'

She sighed a sigh of profound sadness. 'It's a long story…'

'Better start at the beginning,' he said wearily. 'That is, if I really need to know the details of your past with my brother.'

'It really isn't what you think,' she said, her voice not quite steady.

She pushed herself up from the table, paced the distance between the sideboard and the windows, put her hand on her forehead in a gesture that should have seemed overly dramatic but somehow made him sympathise with her.

He didn't get up. 'The beginning,' he prompted, leaning back in his chair. Resting stern face felt entirely appropriate.

'I met Wil when I was thirteen. He was my friend.'

Ned sat forward again. He frowned. 'But Wil was in foster care then.'

Freya didn't meet his gaze, rather looked down somewhere towards her sexy purple suede shoes that tied around her ankles. 'So was I,' she said.

'You were in foster care?' He couldn't keep the shock from his voice. 'Not that there is anything to be...er...ashamed of.'

He knew from Wil, when his brother had finally opened up to him, that there were both good and bad foster homes. Wil's experiences, after being orphaned at five years old, had not been good. His tales from the dark side of state care had only made Ned care all the more for his adopted brother, to feel fiercely protective towards him.

Finally Freya looked towards him. 'I was the girl he defended against our predatory foster father. Wil warned me against him. Protected me. When the horrible guy tried to… to…attack me, Wil pulled him away from me, fought him and broke his nose. Wil got in terrible trouble for doing that—he got sent away. Thankfully for me, a case worker believed Wil when he said I was in danger, and I was taken away from that house. The next foster family was still horrible but I was safer. I… I never saw Wil again after that. But I've always been so grateful to him.'

Ned pushed back his chair, stood up, kept his distance from her, not sure if he could believe her. 'But that girl's name wasn't Freya, it was Tegan.'

Freya looked at him incredulously. 'You know of her? I mean *me*?'

'You're Tegan?' Ned's head was reeling.

'My real name is Freya. That foster mother didn't like it. She insisted on calling me Tegan. Punished me if I didn't answer to it.'

Slowly, Ned shook his head. 'Wil told us about Tegan.'

Her eyes widened. 'Really?'

Ned nodded. 'He tells it just like you do. By protecting Tegan, he got himself into big trouble. The man didn't press charges for assault. But Wil says it was an unforgivable crime for a child to attack a foster parent. He was never placed in foster care again. Instead he was sent to an institution, which he hated. By his account, he was angry and bitter at the way he'd been treated when all he'd done was protect a vulnerable young girl from abuse.'

'That girl is still so grateful to him. Always will be. So...so how did Wil end up in your family? I've often wondered what happened to him.'

'No one told you?'

'Not a word.' Her mouth turned down. 'They told me it was my fault a decent man had his reputation smeared.' She looked up at Ned. 'He was *not* a decent man.'

'So Wil told me.'

Freya looked slight and vulnerable now. He could only imagine how she had been as a terrified thirteen-year-old. Anger flooded through him. He would have broken the man's nose too.

'I can't believe Wil told you about me, that he remembered.'

'Over the years he tried to find you, to see if you were okay. I guess if he was searching for Tegan, that might have been why he had no luck.'

'If only I'd known.' She paused. 'There was nothing between us, you know. Nothing... romantic. We were friends. Both trying to survive in a horrid situation.'

'I believe Wil thought of Tegan as a sister. It would have meant something for him to know you were okay. And there you were, right under our noses, working for my mother's friend.'

'I was helping Hugh to edit Wil's wedding photos when I recognised him. A different surname from when I'd known him, but it was definitely Wil. I didn't tell Hugh. But when he asked me to come out here and do the house shoot, curiosity got the better of me. I wanted to see where Wil had landed so safely.'

'But you must have known he wouldn't be here.'

'Of course, I knew he'd be on his honeymoon. I didn't—don't—want to see him. I can't imagine his wife would welcome someone like me showing up, claiming a shared past. I'm just happy to know everything turned out so well with him. Is Georgia as nice as she seems in her photos?'

'Even nicer. She's a wonderful woman. The best possible wife for him. They're very happy.'

'I'm so glad. My life might have been very different if it wasn't for Wil. It wasn't just that he saved me from that predator, he taught me to be on full alert for any that followed. I was sad to lose him as a friend.'

Ned paused. 'He got sent to an awful residential group home, which is where my parents found him.'

'How did that come about?'

'My parents wanted a big family. But they only had me. They had a lot of love to give. One year they decided to take part in a programme that took needy kids out of residential care and took them home for Christmas. Something about Wil caught their eye. The manager tried to dissuade them, said Wil was a troublemaker. My parents insisted if they couldn't take him, they wouldn't take anyone.'

'How did you feel about that? A strange kid in your home?'

'I'd always wanted a brother. He was hostile at first. But I liked him straight away. I was patient and by the end of those holidays we were firm friends. I was over the moon when we adopted him.'

'He was the troublemaker. You were the peacemaker.'

'If you put it like that, yes.'

'His good deed helping me was rewarded.'

'As a family, we thought it was us who were rewarded.' Life after Wil had been different. Better. He had a brother; his mother became more content with country life once she had another child to lavish love and care on. 'Wil is an extraordinary man.'

'So is his brother,' Freya said, nodding thoughtfully.

Her words unexpectedly warmed him. 'What makes you say that?' he said gruffly.

'Your love for your brother shines through. You never refer to him as your adopted brother.' Her eyes narrowed shrewdly. 'You stepped up when your mother got ill when I suspect you might not have felt ready. You've been very kind to me tonight.'

'But that's just the way I operate.'

'Exactly. Perhaps you don't realise how extraordinary that is. Thank you for believing me.'

He frowned. 'Why would I disbelieve you? Your recollections and Wil's tally perfectly.'

'Not everyone would believe I had no agenda. Your family is very wealthy, for one thing. You might have thought I was after something. I wasn't going to tell you about my connection to Wil. It's not something I've shared with anyone. Even Hugh. But when you asked me to come back and photograph the garden, I knew I had to be honest with you.'

'I appreciate that you did.' He paused. 'But, Freya, there's so much more you're not telling me. About you. Your story. Why you were in state care.'

Freya tugged on that piece of hair again. Gently he reached out and disengaged her fingers. He held onto her hand, small and cool in his much larger hand. Felt an overwhelming urge to protect her. She seemed so strong, but he sensed a deep vulnerability under that smart front.

'It…it's not a particularly pretty story. I'm not sure you want to hear it.'

'I'm very sure that I do,' he said.

Freya had fascinated him from the get-go. He had taken it at face value she had a successful career in a highly competitive business. Hugh and his partner were sophisticated guys and she was close to them. Somehow, he had assumed she'd had a conventional upbringing. He led her by the hand. 'Come on back to the table. Try to eat something. Then share your story with me. Please.'

She shook her head. 'I really would rather not,' she said as she released her hand from his.

Freya had quickly realised that Ned was a kind man. Nurturing too, she suspected. And so good-looking—tonight he was looking especially handsome in a turtleneck cashmere sweater in midnight blue that brought out the blue of his eyes. No wonder she'd had that moment of erotic fantasy over him back in the bedroom of the cottage. Again she wondered why such a man was still single. She could envision him with a bunch of kids. But he was also a son of the squattocracy.

After her first visit she had searched online and discovered there were politicians and entrepreneurs and high-ranking civil servants in his family tree. And wealth, lots of wealth. No wonder prime ministers came to visit.

Her history was so very different she wondered if they could ever connect, even as friends. Henry and his family had certainly thought she was not worthy of being his girlfriend. Not because of her talent or her brains or her personality, but because of her birth and the way she'd been raised. His rejection of her had left a scar, a scar slashed upon the scars of other, older hurts.

She'd met Ned on equal terms. He was the boss of Five and a Half Mile Creek, wealthy beyond her wildest aspirations, and she was in his employ, if only temporarily. But she was highly skilled and provided a creative service he valued—hence her second visit. That put them on an equal footing. Her nanna had cleaned houses for people like his family— how differently might he treat her if he knew that?

She managed to finish half her main course before she pushed her plate away, indicating with a shake of her head that she'd had enough. 'Don't you feel better now for having had something to eat?' he said in a jocular tone that made her smile, in spite of her nervousness.

'Yes,' she said. And she did. She was an erratic eater at the best of times. Hunger made her edgy. She had stopped at a roadhouse for a snack on the way but the offerings had been less than appealing and she'd only managed half of an indifferent burger.

Now with a proper meal inside her she felt stronger. Strong enough to resist the temptation to spill her story to Ned. She did not want his pity. Any semblance of equality between them would be shot if he learned where she came from. She would like to be friends with him. Especially now the truth about her and

Wil was out. But friends needed to meet each other at least halfway on a platform of equality. That platform would be totally shot if he found out where she came from. She couldn't bear to see him turn away from her the way Henry had.

'Can we talk about something else, please?' she said. 'Perhaps tomorrow's garden shoot? The past is not a place I want to step back into too often. I prefer to keep it buried.'

'That's understandable,' he said. But his perceptive blue eyes narrowed. She had a feeling he had further questions to ask. She had no intention of answering them. She pushed back into her chair in an attempt to put more distance between her and Ned.

When the maid brought in the dessert of chocolate-and-raspberry brownies with a bowl of fresh raspberries and cream, and cheese on a marble platter, she welcomed the diversion. And kept the conversation purely on an impersonal level.

CHAPTER FIVE

VERY EARLY THE next morning, Ned stood at a distance, unobserved, watching Freya in his mother's prized rose garden. It was one of the different garden 'rooms'—differentiated, hedged spaces—that led into each other, ending at the boundaries of the orchards that adjoined the entire garden.

The morning was very still and new, the scent from the roses sweet and heady, sharpened by that of the lavender from the borders. Magpies carolled somewhere nearby and a flock of tiny finches were fluttering through one of the larger rose bushes. Freya's presence made the perfect scene appear even more perfect.

She was using a handheld camera to take, he assumed, a close-up of a half-unfurled yellow rose. Again, she wore black jeans, this time with a purple knit sweater against the chill of the morning. Even with sturdy, laced-up boots, she still looked every bit the city girl. Yet she fit. She was meant to be surrounded by flowers, he thought, in one of those odd observations that had come to him from their first moment of meeting.

He was still reeling from her revelations of the night before. The surprising connection with Wil. His shock that she'd been in foster care and in danger. His admiration for his brother shot even higher at the knowledge of his care for that little girl. Wil should be told about the discovery of Tegan. But not by him. It would be up to Freya to decide when to make contact. It was her story, her secret. He knew there was more to her past but she had clammed up when he had tried to find out more about how she'd ended up in state care.

Quite rightly. Her past was really none of his concern. Yet home was so important to him he found it unbearable to think of her shifting from foster placement to foster placement, just a little girl. He admired what she had made of herself after a start like that.

He didn't want to disturb her, so waited until Freya had stepped back from the rose bush and lowered her camera. He took a step forward, his boots crunching on some dried, fallen leaves. Freya whirled immediately around, staring with wide, panicked eyes, then flushed. 'Oh. It's you. I was worried…'

'Worried?'

'Your gardener warned me to keep an eye out for snakes.'

He laughed. 'The gardener was having you on. He picked you for a city slicker and couldn't resist teasing you.'

'He sounded pretty serious to me.' She put her camera down on the large metallic case nearby that held a number of other camera bodies and lenses.

Ned would have a word with the gardener later. There were people you teased about snakes and spiders and there were those you didn't. He wanted Freya to feel comfortable here, not frightened.

'There are snakes in the bush and on our land—it's their home—but we've taken precautions so we don't get them near the house. The lawn is kept short, the bushes trimmed so they don't overhang, no piles of debris allowed to accumulate. There's fine-gauge chicken wire under all the fences around the garden to keep out rabbits and other unwelcome visitors. And see all the gravel pathways? Gravel is sharp. Slithery things don't like it. Besides, they're actually as scared of us as we are of them.'

'Slithery things!' She shuddered. 'I'm hyperventilating at the thought. There are reasons I'm happy being a "city slicker" and snakes are one of them. They terrify me.'

'Most people are frightened of them. My mother is phobic, hence all the precautions. But if you live in a rural area you have to use common sense.'

He wanted to give her a hug, reassure her he was there to protect her from any scary thing that came her way. But after sharing her connection with Wil last night she'd put a barrier up against any overtures of friendship. Their 'goodnights' to each other had been stiffly formal, as appropriate between an employer and contractor. He had no idea if she would welcome a hug from him or push him away.

'Like run a mile if I see one?'

'I promise you won't encounter one in this garden. Just keep stamping your feet when you walk if that makes you feel any better. They don't like vibrations.'

Freya stamped her feet, though even in boots they weren't large or heavy enough to make much of an impact. She laughed. 'I don't think that would scare away so much as a worm.'

'You'd be surprised,' he said, smiling. He liked her resilience, the fact she could laugh at her fears. 'But I'm actually here to warn you about something else—the weather.'

She looked up at the sky. 'The weather app on my phone is playing up. The advance forecast was good but I haven't been able to check it since. Something doesn't feel quite right today.' Ned was surprised at how concerned she seemed.

'It's not looking good for this afternoon. We check against detailed meteorological information. Storms have been forecast.'

Again a frown that didn't seem to be warranted by a conversation about the weather. 'I'd better get a move on, then,' she said. 'This garden is so big. Every time I turn a corner there's more—and then the countryside beyond. It's so beautiful, isn't it? In Melbourne there are parks and open spaces, I love the

Botanical Gardens, but it's not like *this*.' She encompassed her surroundings with a wave. 'I'm getting a real fix of nature.'

'You'll have to come back another time,' he said casually, offhand, no pressure. The connection with Wil was reason enough for her to return. But he wanted to have Freya as *his* friend. For her to come back to *him*, not his brother.

'To see the garden in another season, you mean?'

'That's a point. It's glorious in spring. The wisteria walkway is quite famous. And the daffodils. Plus even more roses. My mother used to open the garden for charity in spring and autumn.'

'Will you carry on the tradition?'

'I've got more than enough on my plate without adding that to it,' he said. Traditionally, the gardens of Five and a Half Mile Creek were the woman's domain.

'Waiting for that wife to come along and take over all that "lady of the manor" stuff?' she asked in a teasing tone, as if she had read his thoughts.

He swallowed hard. 'Is that a trick question?' It veered a bit close to his wife wish-list. Carrying on with those kinds of traditions was exactly what a good country wife would be expected to do.

'No,' she said. 'I'm just interested.'

He shrugged. 'If she wanted to. It would be up to her.'

'Or you could hire an event planner.'

'That's a thought,' he said.

'It seems so surreal to someone like me. Organising charity fundraisers is completely out of my experience.'

'I guess it might be,' he said. One of his mother's favourite charities helped children in need as both Freya and Wil had been—but he didn't want to mention it. 'Surreal indeed.'

She looked up at the sky again, squinting a little against the early morning sun. Her hair glinted pale gold and the tiny jewel in her eyebrow stud glittered. 'I'd better take advantage of the good weather while I've got it. I hope the storm will blow over and we'll have a good day tomorrow.'

'I hope so too. I'll leave you to it.'

He was just about to invite her to lunch at the house when she spoke. 'Do you think I could make a sandwich to bring out here for lunch? I don't want to waste a minute before the weather changes.'

So he wouldn't get to share lunch with her. He fought his disappointment. 'I'll ask Marian to organise it. She makes excellent sandwiches.'

'I'm sure she does, if the other meals I've had here are anything to go by. That would be wonderful, thank you.'

'I'll bring them out to you myself.'

'Oh, that would be wonderful too. But don't you have work to do? The boss of this huge place? I don't want to hold you up.'

'Even the boss has to stop for lunch.' Any excuse to spend time with her. He could catch up after she'd gone and he would have untold hours to himself.

'I guess,' she said.

'I'll see you at midday,' he said, starting to turn away.

'Wait,' she said. 'You're so thoughtful. I appreciate it.' She smiled that gap-toothed smile he found so enchanting.

'No problem,' he said. She seemed to take

common courtesy as something out of the ordinary.

'Before you go.' She put up her hand to stop him again, then paused. 'While you're taking orders, no pickles, please.'

Ned smiled and turned to go, happier than he should be that he would be seeing her again at lunchtime. He would have to reschedule the work he had planned for that time. And think about how he could get Freya out here for a third visit after the garden assignment was done.

Freya liked Ned more each time she saw him. Watching him as he walked away, she could not help but admire—again—that stupendous back view. But it wasn't just about how hot she found him. It was about the person he was proving himself to be. She'd dreaded telling him about her connection with Wil, feared his reaction to her revelation she'd been in foster care. Horrible Henry's reaction had been an ill-disguised disgust.

Last night at dinner, she *had* seen disgust on Ned's face. But that had been when he'd thought she had some kind of ulterior motive in revealing her past with Wil. It had been followed by kindness and understanding. She had meant it when she had told Ned his face was open and easy to read. Easy for someone like her, anyway, who had had to learn from a tender age who she could trust, who she had to be wary of.

Last night she had seen Ned look at her with dismay as a duplicitous potential blackmailer, destroyer of his brother's marriage, possible gold-digger. There had been something else too. Something that she hadn't been able to place until later.

Disappointment.

Ned had been unable to mask his disappointment that she seemed to be interested—perhaps even obsessed with—his brother, which would cut Ned right out of the picture with her. It was so not true. Wil was movie-star handsome, had been stunningly good-looking and very manly, even at thirteen. But she had never been attracted to heartthrob Wil. It was conservative, kind, gorgeous Ned who had her heartbeat accelerating when he was nearby and her mind indulging in wild sensual fantasies when he was not.

* * *

Ned brought her a sandwich—no pickles—
for lunch, along with a thoughtful selection
of drinks and some fruit. He also brought
lunch for himself and they enjoyed a quick,
impromptu picnic under the shade of a glorious camellia studded with exquisite pale pink
blooms. In the brief time they had for conversation, he filled her in on some of the history
of the farm and his Scottish ancestors who'd
originally settled the place.

During the conversation she'd had to force
herself not to wonder how Ned would look
in a kilt. Tall, brawny, reddish glints in his
hair—he fitted the part. She could not, would
not, allow her thoughts to stray to whether or
not he would go commando under the kilt.
Friends did not let their thoughts stray in that
direction.

Then she got back to her work and he to his.

Now the afternoon light was fading, the
threatened storm had rumbled, spat down
some rain, and held off. The air felt still, heav-
ily charged, uncertain. It worried her; she and
storms did not do well together. She had shot
as much of the autumn garden as she could,

anticipating it might not be good conditions the next day. It was such a thoughtful gift for Ned to arrange for his mother, she wanted to do not just a good job but an excellent one.

She was struck by a pang of longing for Nanna, whose memory faded with each year Freya moved away from being twelve. She dreaded the day she couldn't remember her at all; she only had a few photos left, which she'd managed to hang onto through her years in care.

But one of her strongest memories of the woman who had mothered her was of her grandmother in her tiny scrap of a front yard, tending the red rose she had trained along the cast-iron lacework of the narrow front veranda of the single-level terrace.

Nanna had nurtured that rose, the old lemon tree, and the bed of white daisies that had made up her garden. Once she'd lost her leg to diabetes she couldn't work in it any more, hadn't wanted to. And Freya hadn't known what to do to help her. One of the reasons she'd returned to the area to live was that for a long time the old house had remained the same, and the climbing rose had lived on. Its tenacity had given her some comfort, some continuity. But gentrification had finally struck. Last time she'd driven past the house it had been gutted, modernised and the rose ripped out.

Ned would understand if she shared that memory with him, she realised. Might even give her one of his wonderful hugs. No matter how many times she told herself he wasn't her type, she found herself more and more attracted to him. Now she knew the feeling didn't run one way. That look of disappointment when he'd thought she was a former girlfriend of Wil's had confirmed it.

But Ned had said he wanted to get married, have kids; he had 'family man' stamped all over him. While she was a no-strings type of girl who never wanted to marry or have children. He wasn't the kind of guy to have a fling with—especially as there was a good chance she might have further meetings with him and his family. She wanted to see Wil, meet Georgia and baby Nina. It had been heart-warming and, somehow, healing to know that Wil had remembered Tegan.

She couldn't allow herself to get closer to Ned. Much as she was aching to do just that.

It would have been sensible to say 'no' to his invitation to another dinner with him at the house this evening. The kitchen in the cottage was stocked with a few basics—she wouldn't go hungry if she said she was tired after a long day and stayed there. But, yet…she couldn't get her 'yes' out quickly enough.

CHAPTER SIX

THE RAIN HAD started in earnest as Freya had finished packing up her equipment. By the time she was dressed and ready for dinner with Ned at the house, it was coming down in torrents. Fortunately, the cottage was well supplied with all creature comforts—including a selection of folding umbrellas.

But the flimsy umbrella she chose was no match for the wind that gusted the slanting rain right at her the second she stepped out of the door. As she fought it along the pathway to the house, she questioned the wisdom of having worn her favourite purple suede shoes instead of boots thanks to an impulse to look her best for Ned. He probably wouldn't even notice.

The rain was coming down so hard it had driven channels into the gravel, forming small gushing streams. The path was well lit, but it was getting more difficult to avoid the streams and save her shoes and she found herself jumping from side to side as if in a game of aquatic hopscotch. She cursed out loud when the umbrella suddenly turned completely inside out. She was left with only a light jacket over her dress for protection against the elements.

Then Ned was there. 'Seems like you could do with some help,' he said. He was sensibly encased in a long oilskin raincoat and held aloft an enormous black umbrella.

'This darn umbrella is useless,' she spluttered and threw it on the ground.

'Don't tell me—you chose it because it was purple.'

'It was the first one I saw,' she fibbed. Of course she'd been attracted to the pattern of purple iris. The possible sturdiness of the umbrella hadn't been a consideration.

'Come here,' he said. 'You don't want to ruin those sexy shoes.'

Had he said '*sexy*' shoes?

In the split second she took to consider his choice of words, Ned had pulled her to him and under the shelter of his umbrella. Suddenly the stinging onslaught of the rain on her face stopped, but she was far too distracted by Ned's closeness to care. She was dry. She was warm.

He was hot.

'It's great to get rain. We need it. Trouble is when it all comes down like this at once, so much of it runs off.'

'Hopefully it will ease off,' she said.

His chest was a wall of solid muscle. As he led her towards the house, steering her through the channels, she leaned in closer. Just, of course, to make sure she was completely under the shelter of his umbrella.

'We're almost there or I'd pick you up and carry you,' he said.

'What?'

'You're a little thing. Nowhere as heavy as a full-grown sheep to sling over my shoulder.'

Before she had a chance to reply, they reached the house. In one fluid movement, Ned ditched his umbrella, put his hands under her armpits, lifted her off the ground and up the steps, depositing her on the veranda. Freya was back on her feet, out of the rain, before she had time to protest.

'Did you just compare me to a sheep?' she said, mock glaring up at him, a smile twitching at the corners of her mouth. His hair was dark with damp and fat drops of water sat on his cheeks. He grinned. Her heart gave that curious lurch of recognition—she didn't know where it came from.

'A ewe, if I'm to be precise,' he said.

'I'm glad you at least amended that to be a lady sheep.' She couldn't resist his grin and responded with one of her own. 'Do you really lift and haul sheep around the place?' If so, no wonder the man was made of muscle.

'If needs be,' he said. 'I grew up learning to do everything that needed to be done with sheep. Rescue them, shear them, sometimes birth them. So, yeah, I've had to haul around the odd sheep or two over the years. No special treatment for the boss.'

He sounded so laconic, so laid-back, so *manly* she leaned up on tiptoe and kissed him on the cheek. 'Thank you, for rescuing me like a stray sheep caught in the rain.' She froze.

Why did she do that?

Her lips tingled from the connection to his skin, cool with raindrops. For a crazy moment she'd wanted to taste them, taste *him*. Her gaze connected with his for a long, still moment.

The rain drummed on the roof of the veranda, splashed out of the overflowing guttering onto the garden beds below that bordered it. It released a green, earthy scent she was never aware of in the city.

'It was truly my pleasure,' he said slowly. He reached down and, with a touch that was very tender for such a big man, swiped under her eyes with his thumb, first one and then the other. 'Your make-up is smeared.'

She shivered with awareness of his touch, hoped he wouldn't notice, or he would blame it on the chill of the rain and her damp jacket.

'I… I must look like a drowned rat. Or…or sheep.'

'You look like a beautiful woman who has been caught in the rain,' he said in that deep, resonant voice.

'I… I should do something about it, get tissues or something.' She looked up into his eyes. They seemed to darken a further shade of blue as he looked back down at her.

'Yeah,' he said.

Still she didn't move. Neither did Ned.

Her gaze dropped from his eyes to his

mouth. Such a beautiful mouth for a man: firm, sculpted, generous.

How would it feel on hers?

She felt herself swaying towards him, her lips parting in anticipation.

Not a good move.

A kiss on the mouth was a very different matter from a kiss on the cheek. A kiss on the mouth would take her across a line where she shouldn't go. Friendship with Ned was something she could handle. Anything else was a no-go zone. Especially when they were so very, very different.

Ned stepped closer. She ached to raise her face for his kiss. But it would be wrong.

This could go nowhere.

Freya felt suddenly seized by panic that she could so easily be overwhelmed by the desire to be close to this man. She forced herself to step back, broke the gaze, extinguished that dancing spark of awareness that had hovered between them from the get-go.

She wrapped her arms around her torso, blocking him out. 'I'm feeling chilled—'

He didn't hesitate. 'We need to get you inside to dry off.'

He took a few long strides to the door, flung it open, ushered her inside. Without a steering arm on her elbow. Without touching.

Hands off.

She should feel relieved instead of bereft.

The grand house felt immediately warm and welcoming, with lamps glowing on tables, a hint of the scent of wood-smoke. 'There are towels and a hairdryer in the powder room,' he said. 'When you're ready, come down to the kitchen. You know the way.'

'Thank you,' she said. She looked up at him. 'Ned?'

'Yes?'

'You were right. I did choose that useless umbrella because it had purple flowers on it.'

'I knew it,' he said, with another of those grins that warmed her as much as the central heating in the house. 'Soon you'll have no secrets from me.' A smile stayed on his face as he turned away to stride down that magnificent hallway.

Freya's smile slipped. There were secrets she would never share. Her family history for one. Dark times she had struggled to get through.

How could a man like Ned, who came from such privilege, ever understand?

As she looked in the bathroom mirror to check for signs of damage, she wiped away a raindrop sliding down her cheek and was horrified to realise it was a teardrop. Ned had come into her life totally unexpectedly. She liked him more with each minute. But she couldn't have him. He wasn't what she wanted. She certainly wasn't what he needed.

Friends, Freya. Think friends. That's all it can be.

Ned now knew that Freya didn't like pickles. But he didn't know any more of her dietary likes and dislikes. It wasn't the kind of thing he'd thought to ask. There were more important things he wanted to know about her. Like, was there a boyfriend in Melbourne? She'd said she wasn't married or engaged. But that didn't mean he didn't have competition.

Competition for what?

Ned pulled himself up short. He shouldn't be thinking of anything that even hinted at a relationship with Freya. She didn't check one box on his wife wish-list. As well, she thought his home was 'too far from civilisation'—the busy, frantic city she loved and he had come to loathe. But in spite of that, since that day the previous week that she'd flitted into his life, his days were filled with thoughts of her. He intended to enjoy her company while he could.

It was his staff's night off so it was to be an informal meal tonight. He hoped Freya would like the fillet of beef Marian had prepared. His housekeeper had put it in the oven just before he'd set off to see if Freya was okay coming up from the cottage in the rain. Some nagging thought had told him she might need help.

Freya had looked both forlorn and cranky with that silly umbrella, and his protective instincts had been aroused. Feelings of an altogether different kind had been aroused by holding her close and from that sweet, simple kiss on the cheek. An insignificant gesture to have had such an effect on him.

He'd ached to follow it up with a proper kiss but had been held back by the instinct that he had to take it easy with Freya. She was like an injured wild animal he knew took patience to tame. Not that she was injured—not physically anyway—or indeed wild, although there was an appealing feistiness to her. But she might be emotionally damaged as Wil had been by his past. She needed careful handling, a cautious approach. Even if a friendship was all that would evolve from their unexpected meeting as they were two total opposites.

He took the beef out of the oven to rest before serving it. 'That smells so good,' Freya said as she came into the kitchen. 'Did you prepare all this?'

She indicated the dishes on the countertop, then lifted the lid from a pan of mushrooms in a garlic-and-cream sauce. For a moment he was tempted to say 'yes' to impress her, but he would soon be caught out.

'Can't claim credit for any of it, although I did choose the wine. I can cook basic stuff but this is all Marian's work. She's made a brilliant creamy mash with truffle oil and a selection of vegetables from the garden. All we have to do is heat it up.' Ned had studiously ignored his housekeeper's blatant comments about what a lovely girl Freya was and how she hoped they'd see her more often at Five and a Half Mile Creek. As if he needed reminding.

'Sounds as good as any restaurant in Melbourne. Will Marian join us for dinner?'

He shook his head. For one thing, he didn't fraternise with staff—something he needed to remind himself of sooner or later. 'She lives with her husband in their apartment in the staff accommodation.'

'So it's just us?' she said.

'You okay with that?'

'Sure,' she said. But there was an edge to her voice he wasn't sure how to interpret. Had she been as unsettled as he had been by their moment on the veranda? Holding her close had been mind-blowing. It had taken all his willpower not to pull her into his arms and kiss her thoroughly. But he would wait for his cue from her. Once started, kissing wouldn't be enough.

She was enchanting, this quirky city girl. He found it difficult to keep his eyes off her, to stop them from roaming her body to take in every detail. Her lovely face—all water damage now repaired, though she'd looked very cute in drowned-rat mode—her hair dry and sleek again and falling below her shoulders. Her curves, hugged by a dark purple dress, the colour of blackberries, and those sexy, sexy shoes tied with suede ribbons around her ankles.

'I don't know about you, but getting caught in the rain has made me hungry,' he said.

'I suspect a big guy like you might always be hungry,' she said. 'Carrying all those sheep around must help build up an appetite.'

He laughed. 'You might be right.'

Freya carried the platter with the beef on it over to the table in the dining area. Ned followed with more dishes. She stopped, platter still in hand, and called back to him over her shoulder. 'The…the dog is in here.' Her voice rose on the last words.

Ned muttered a curse. 'Molly. Sorry. I forgot to put her out.'

He followed Freya's anxious gaze to where his black-and-white dog lay stretched out full-length on her rug in front of the very smart wood-burning heater that had been installed as part of the renovation. He liked real flames as well as central heating. At the sound of her name, Molly opened one eye—the unclouded one—thumped her tail a few times, heaved a doggy sigh, and settled back down.

'She's pretending to be asleep,' Ned said. 'Hoping I'll leave her there toasting in front of the fire.'

'Is she really that smart?' He noticed Freya had moved from referring to his dog as 'it' to 'she'. A step in the right direction.

'Border collies are very smart dogs, and she's a very smart border collie. She's also very old and frightened of storms.'

'Frightened of storms?'

'Thunder in particular.'

Freya looked down at Molly, her expression again difficult to read. 'I'm frightened of storms myself.'

'You're also terrified of dogs. Don't worry, I'll take her out.'

'Outside? In the wet? In the cold?' she said.

'She does have a big kennel on the veranda.'

'It would be horrible out there for her.'

'Which is why I'll lock her in the utility room.'

'No! Don't do that.' Freya looked nervously across at Molly. 'She's not doing anything scary. Just lying there.'

Molly let out a convincing doggy snore. 'Fast asleep, in fact,' Ned said. Clever Molly.

'She's ignoring me, as if I wasn't in the room.'

'Just obeying orders. I told her to stay away from you.'

'Perhaps…perhaps you should leave her there.'

'If you're sure you're okay with it?'

'I think I'm pretty safe over here. And she… she's safe from the storm.'

'Thank you on my dog's behalf,' he said. 'She'd thank you herself but she's not quite *that* smart.'

Freya put the platter on the table. 'But I remain on this side of the room and the dog remains on the other.'

'Agreed,' he said. 'And now to get down to the serious business of eating.'

He would reward Molly with a slice of roast beef later. And he might concede to Freya a scrap of his 'must love animals' wife requirement. Because even though she was frightened of Molly, she'd shown empathy towards his dog. Surely that counted? Or was he clutching at straws because he wanted Freya to fit in here? For them to have even the tiniest patch of common ground on which to meet?

CHAPTER SEVEN

FREYA DIDN'T MAKE friends easily. Her friends were often more akin to acquaintances, with Freya unwilling—subconsciously or not—to make the emotional commitment to trust somebody that true friendship required. She suspected this was a hangover from her years in state care. To get too close to another kid in foster care or a residential home usually ended with a move for one of them, sometimes without the opportunity to say goodbye. That was how it had been with Wil.

As a result, she had just a few good friends. They included a girl she'd met at uni, now a graphic designer living not far from her in Melbourne; another girl who'd been a receptionist at Hugh's studio when Freya had started as his assistant, now an account manager in one of the big advertising agencies; and of course Hugh and his partner, Gordon, who she sometimes felt were as close to family as she had in her life.

So she marvelled at how at ease she felt with Ned, as if they were friends of long-standing duration. In fact, she had friends she had never felt this level of connection with. One thing in particular stood out—she didn't need to consider her words before she spoke in her conversations with Ned. Overthinking before she opened her mouth was another habit she'd got into while in care, for self-preservation purposes.

With some of the foster families she'd been with, you never knew what the consequences of the 'wrong' answer might be—like admitting she was frightened of storms. Apparently that was something exceedingly immature, which had to be 'worked through', in the words of one cruel foster mother. It wasn't so much the rain, it was the thunder, the lightning, the utter out-of-control violence of a storm that scared her. You'd think an adult would have understood that and been kind to a terrified thirteen-year-old who'd just been sent—again—to live with strangers.

Ned was so darn kind he even considered

the feelings of his dog. No way could Freya have allowed him to boot the poor animal out into the cold. If she'd insisted he would have done so, but how would he have felt about her as a consequence?

Their dinner conversation centred again around the history of Five and a Half Mile Creek. She heard how it had once been even bigger, but over the years land had been hived off and new homesteads built to accommodate second and third sons; how electricity and telephone connections had come early to the property, thanks to past Hudson members of parliament. Again, she marvelled at the long history and connection Ned had to this land. Such an enviable legacy of security and certainty.

But she heard nothing that led her closer to personal knowledge of this man who, despite her best resolutions to stamp down on her attraction, continued to intrigue her. He wanted to know *her* secrets, what about *his*? Why wasn't a super-eligible guy like Ned married, or in a permanent relationship? A friend could ask those kinds of personal questions, couldn't she? Especially if she was emboldened by the very good red wine he had served with the beef.

She decided on a roundabout way of questioning him. 'You'd make a good father, Ned,' she said as she nibbled on the flaky apple pastry his housekeeper had made for dessert.

Ned nearly choked on his pastry. He had to pick up his glass of water and gulp some down before he could speak. 'What makes you say that?' he spluttered.

'The way you are with Molly, for one thing.'

He laughed. 'She's a working dog, not a child substitute.'

'Not all working dogs get to loll in front of a fire and be fed roast beef when their master is pretending to stoke the fire.'

'You noticed?' She found his caught-out expression endearing.

'I pretended not to. It was too cute the way you were both being so sneaky.'

'When I was a kid it was a strict rule not to feed dogs at the table. I thought I'd learned to be surreptitious about breaking that particular edict. Because break it I did, many times over the years. My dogs were my best friends.' He glanced over at Molly as if enlisting her support. Freya found that endearing too. As a matter of fact, there was a lot she found endearing about Ned Hudson.

She rather liked the idea of being on his side. 'Where you fed her wasn't strictly the table, was it? It was her rug. And don't you get to make your own rules around here now, bossman?'

He smiled. 'I like the way you're complicit with my rule breaking and setting.'

'I'm all for it,' she said. 'I'm sure Molly would agree.'

His voice softened. 'She's a good dog. An excellent companion.'

Freya hesitated. Decided to go ahead. Took another sip of red wine to fuel her bravado. 'But a dog isn't the same as a person.'

'True. But if you remember, until I was fourteen and Wil came along, I was an only child. There was a lack of companions my own age and the adults were usually too busy to give me much time. When I wasn't away at boarding school, my dog and my horses were my friends.'

Her heart turned over at the thought of the sweet young boy Ned must have been with his animal friends. It made a poignant image. Perhaps his life hadn't been as story-book perfect as she'd imagined.

'Even with Molly for company, you must get lonely in this big house.'

'Most of the time I'm too busy to be lonely.' He paused. 'But, yeah, I am on my own a lot. Not how I planned it, but how it's turned out.'

Freya knew she should probably leave it at that, but she wanted to know more. 'What's your story, Ned? How come you're on your own when you're pushing thirty?'

He picked up his wine, looked at her over the rim of the glass. 'I could ask the same of you.'

'You could, but I asked you first.'

'Fair enough.' He took a sip from his wine, put it back down. 'Timing, probably. Right person at the wrong time. Or just the wrong person.'

'Was it just timing? I'm surprised you're by yourself. You...you seem the marrying kind to me.'

Ned's laugh was more of a snort of incredulity than anything humorous. 'What do you mean by that?'

Freya clenched her hand around the stem

of her glass. Why had she thought this was a good line of conversation to initiate? 'I can't really put it into words. But I meant it in a good way. I can imagine you with a...a devoted wife and a brood of kids.' She stumbled on the 'devoted wife' bit, as she knew it was something she could never be to a man, no matter how much she wanted him.

'Why is that?'

'For a start, you're kind, caring, family orientated.' She could add 'solid, reliable, grounded in good values' but decided she'd gone far enough already. Besides, she didn't know that of him for sure.

Ned sat back in his chair. 'Hey. That all makes me sound kinda boring. How about adventurous? Fearless? A risk-taker?' He beat on his chest with his fists in a Tarzan-like display of strength. Under his light navy-blue sweater, his muscles rippled.

She laughed. 'All those too.'

'You could be right, though,' he said thoughtfully. 'In fact, I wanted to get married when I was eighteen.'

'*Eighteen?* Who gets married at eighteen?'

'An infatuated teenager?'

'That sounds about right.'

'It seemed very real at the time. She felt the same. Although, looking back, I can see the relationship would have been a disaster.'

'I'm intrigued, please tell all.' She was intrigued, but she was also more than a touch disconcerted at how distasteful she found the thought of Ned with another woman. Even when he was eighteen years old. This pretending to be 'just friends' with a man you were desperately attracted to wasn't as easy as she had anticipated. 'You must still have been at school.'

'Boarding school in Melbourne, my final year.' He named the most prestigious private boys' school in the state. 'Teresita was at our "sister" girls' school. Not that we saw much of the girls, except when it was deemed socially advantageous for us to get together.'

'I bet they fought to keep you apart,' she said. 'It seems so old-fashioned to have single-sex schools.'

To be fair, though, she'd liked the segregated, all-girls residential institution in which she'd spent her final years in care because she'd felt safer there. At her co-ed high school, she'd tried to avoid the boys. Even to the point of starving herself to minimise the curves that brought unwanted attention. There had been no high-school boyfriends for her. She'd met her first, older boyfriend at university. Hadn't discovered until it was all over that he'd been notorious for preying on 'freshers'.

'I don't know that I'd send any kid of mine to a single-sex school,' Ned said.

Freya nearly said *me neither*—but she had no intention of ever having kids.

'So how did you meet your girlfriend?' she said instead. 'Your first girlfriend, right?'

'The schools had a joint orchestra. I met Teresita at rehearsals. She was a really talented musician. We hit if off immediately. Then we…we…'

'Fell in love?' she prompted. It was an effort to make her voice impartial when she thought of Ned falling crazily in love.

'Yes, we snuck out to meet whenever we could.'

'You're a musician? Those instruments in the music room are yours?'

'The grand piano is a family heirloom. I learned to play on it. But the violin was my instrument. If you saw Wil's wedding video you'd have seen me playing fiddle in the bush band.'

'I haven't seen it.' She made a mental memo to get hold of the video when she got back to Melbourne.

'I particularly enjoy playing the Celtic fiddle—foot-tapping, hand-clapping. But classical was what we played in the school orchestra.'

'You're a man of many talents. I'm impressed.'

The more she knew of Ned, the more impressed she became. There'd been no opportunity for her to learn to play a musical instrument. Music lessons were optional, expensive extras at the various schools she had attended. And the cost of an instrument—even the hire of one—prohibitive.

'Her diplomat parents were not impressed with me. When they found out that Teresita and I were together, they put an end to it. They made communication between us impossible. Then when our final exams were over, they whisked her home to the Philippines.'

'Did you see her again?'

'Never.' A note of bitterness sharpened his

voice. Freya didn't blame him for it. He and his girlfriend had been old enough to be in love and plan a life together and had been treated like naughty children. The same way she had had to submit to the authority of people who hadn't always had her best interests at heart.

'I'm sorry. That must have been heartbreaking.'

'Not that a guy that age would easily admit to it, but yeah. I tried to contact her. Her phone was disconnected. The email address I had for her bounced.'

He looked down at the table, hiding his expression.

'I'm sorry,' she said, feeling the words were inadequate.

He looked up again. 'In hindsight, her parents were probably right. We were young and naïve. Didn't have anything much in common except music. We both had family obligations that governed our futures.'

'It would have been good if you'd been allowed to figure that out for yourself.'

'Yes, it would've. My parents didn't like me getting so serious so young either, but they didn't intervene. However, as I still had university to get through, I suspect they heaved a sigh of relief when Teresita flew home.'

Freya was glad of the opportunity to segue to a less fraught topic. 'What did you study at uni?'

'Agri-business at Melbourne. The degree equipped me for the role I knew was to come. From when I was a kid I wanted to be a vet, but that went by the board.'

'I could see you as a vet, you love animals so much. So why didn't that happen?'

'To study veterinary science was at least six years at uni. That meant a lot of time away from home and little opportunity to actually practise if I qualified, except on our own animals. Wil wasn't interested in farming. Dad needed me here.'

'Did you want to be here?' She thought she detected a trace of disappointment at having to give up his dream.

He raised his brows. 'I never resented the choice I made. I liked what I studied and it helped me modernise the way things are run here. It was a good path to take.'

Freya took another sip of her wine. It was all very well to hear about his qualifications.

But she was becoming obsessed with his dating history. This might be the only chance she got to find out.

'What about at uni? You must have broken a few hearts there.'

He shook his head. 'I didn't break any hearts.' He said it so seriously, so sincerely, like the gentleman he was. 'Not that I was aware of, anyway. I had a girlfriend I met in second year. She came from up Moree way, in central New South Wales. Her family grew cotton on a big scale.'

Jealousy—ridiculous, unwarranted, irrational—speared Freya. That girlfriend was the right kind of woman for man-of-the-land Ned. The type he would marry to get that doting wife and brood of kids. His own kind. He wasn't her type, either, she had to remind herself yet again. They came from different worlds—she could no more imagine Ned living in inner-city Melbourne than she could imagine herself living here, in spite of his story of busking in the city.

'What happened?'

'We both went back to our respective properties at vacation time. Had to start over again back at uni.'

'She was a term-time girlfriend?'

'Pretty much. After we graduated, it just fizzled out. We kept in touch. She's married now.'

Good. 'And after her was—?' Surely he had a more up-to-date girlfriend story to share?

'This is quite the interrogation,' he said with that slow smile, his way of looking into her eyes, that felt as intimate as a touch. 'I hope you're going to be as forthcoming when I turn the tables on you.'

She flushed. 'Er...of course. Not much to tell from my side. I'm a dating disaster zone. I... I don't have what it takes to make relationships work. Not for long anyway.'

'I find that difficult to believe.' He narrowed his eyes and she was intensely aware of his scrutiny, that he liked what he saw. 'Perhaps you haven't met the right man?'

Because she always went for the wrong ones.

She'd tried with Henry but he'd turned out to be as much a dud as the self-centred musician, or the lying fellow photography student at uni. Besides, what was the point? She didn't want to get married or even live with a guy.

Her independence and emotional equilibrium were too important. The good part of her life had only started when she had been able to take control of them. She had no intention of relinquishing her heart.

'Let's get back to you,' she said. 'You're far more interesting.'

'As long as I get equal time to question you,' he said. 'In fact, I'll trade question for question. Do you have a boyfriend in Melbourne?'

For a moment she was thrown. 'No,' she said. 'I haven't dated for six months.'

'Six months? What's wrong with the men in Melbourne?'

She had to smile at that. Almost replied, *They're not like you.* Realised that would sound provocative. 'Maybe they're not worth bothering about,' she said, too glibly. 'I've been working long hours, sometimes away on location, no time for dating.' She deflected him with another question. 'What about you?'

He shrugged. 'Living out here it's not easy to meet women. I've dated off and on. There was one woman I liked a lot. I met her at a trade show in Melbourne. We seemed to have a lot in common. Had a lot of fun on my visits to the city. But she turned out to be not the person I thought she was.'

His mouth tightened to a bitter line. This was the one, Freya thought, the one who had broken his heart and had him hiding way out here at the back of nowhere.

'Was it because she didn't want to live out here so far from—?'

'Civilisation?' he finished for her with a weary note to his voice.

'Actually, I meant so far away from Melbourne.'

'That was part of it. I had to make a choice between her and Five and a Half Mile Creek. Her behaviour made that choice easy.'

'Did she—?'

'I don't wish to discuss it further.' His tone made it very clear the conversation was closed.

'I understand,' she said. 'And I'm sorry about another *too far from civilisation* gaffe from me.'

'It was also a saying of my mother's, so it's a bit like the screech of chalk on a blackboard to me.'

'But from what you said, she had a wonderful life with her garden and her fundraising parties and living in this beautiful house.' She waved her arm to encompass the room and the rooms beyond it.

'It wasn't quite like that.'

That wasn't the reply she'd expected. Freya realised Ned's mouth had set in a grim line and he had abandoned all attempt at finishing his dessert. So had she. She had fought her curves for so long, merely tasting a dessert to be polite had become a habit.

'What do you mean?' she said tentatively.

'All that wasn't enough for my mother. I don't know the ins and outs of my parents' marriage, but apparently the novelty of living out here wore off pretty quickly.'

'But you said your parents were madly in love.'

Freya struggled to assimilate this new information, so discordant with the picture she'd built up of Ned's life at Five and a Half Mile Creek. She didn't want to be disillusioned. She loved to hear about happy endings, there'd been so few in her life.

'I think they were very happy for the first few years. But farming isn't a nine-to-five job. My father wasn't around much. My mother had given up a very successful career. Once she'd completely redesigned every room she could get her hands on here, she got bored. Before long she'd started accepting commissions in Melbourne and spending weeks at a time away from here.'

'What happened to you when your mother went to Melbourne for work?'

'When I was little she took me with her and her parents looked after me. As I got older I wanted to stay here. I hated going to Melbourne. When I started school in Hilltop, she couldn't pull me out of class on a whim.'

Freya shook her head slowly from side to side. 'Ned, I don't know what to say. I'd pictured a perfect, idyllic childhood for you here.'

'It was all that, while my mother was around.' His eyes darkened with what she thought was remembered sadness. 'She called us every night, but I was miserable those times Mum went to Melbourne for weeks on end. I couldn't understand why she wanted to leave me and Dad on our own. And Dad, desperately unhappy himself, couldn't ease up on the work just because I was there. He hired nannies to care for me but no one could replace my mother.'

'Of course you would have been miserable.' Freya remembered how devastated she had been when Nanna had to go into hospital and she had had to first live with strangers. 'Wait.' She put up her hand in a halt sign. 'Didn't you say you lived with Hugh and Gordon for a while?'

'When I was nine my parents separated. Mum went back to Melbourne for good. I had to go with Mum as I was so young.'

'I'm sorry, Ned.' Again she felt her words were inadequate.

He locked his hands together on the table so his knuckles showed pale. 'You know last night you said you didn't like to revisit the past? I'm the same. I don't remember a lot of that time, just how much I hated it. I don't *want* to remember it. I was wrenched away from everything I loved. Had to change schools and live in Brunswick—' he spat out the name of the lively, inner-city Melbourne suburb as if it were something loathsome '—when I was used to the run of Five and a Half Mile Creek. I missed my dog, my horse, my home. Melbourne was so far away, I only got a visit from my dad every two weeks.'

Freya wished she could hug that homesick little boy. Heck, she wished she could hug the twenty-nine-year-old man. She wondered if that enforced separation had scored deep scars of pain and loss. Could that be the real reason the family man was still single? But with every word of his story, her spirits were sinking lower. He was even more of a country boy than she had thought. And she was a rural misfit.

'That's so sad,' she said, instead of the hug. 'But your parents seem well and truly together now.'

He unclenched his hands, she was relieved to see. 'For six months I lived with Mum in Melbourne. But, the story goes, she was as miserable as I was. She missed Dad and she realised she missed a lot about Five and a Half Mile Creek. Dad says he got his act together and delegated more of the running of the property to managers. He spent more time with my mother. There's always been a garden near the house. But that was when Mum went all out to expand and create new areas. She brought in top horticulturalists to help her make it the award-winning garden it is today. Dad worked alongside her. He once told me they'd never stopped loving each other. When she came home, it was for good.'

'And it was for you too.'

He paused. 'Do you remember the lucky horseshoe in my study?'

'With ends right way up to catch the good luck?'

'I kept that horseshoe by my bedside the entire time I was away, to remind me of Five and a Half Mile Creek. It went to boarding school and university with me too.'

'Seems like it worked. The good luck, I mean.'

'I don't like to think of myself as superstitious. But during that time in exile in Melbourne, I remember wishing so hard for what seemed like the impossible—a brother or a sister.'

Freya had to clear her throat against a sudden lump of emotion. 'Your wish came true.'

'Big time. Everything got better when Wil came into our lives. I finally got a brother. My mother got another son to focus her maternal energies on. Wil needed a lot of love and attention and my parents were the right people to give them to him. I remember the hours my dad and I spent teaching him to ride a horse, teaching him about trust.'

'You had a lot of love to give too.' Wil had hit the brother jackpot with Ned. Seemed Ned thought the same about Wil.

'He's the best brother any guy could have,' he said. 'Now I also have a wonderful sister-in-law and a cute little niece.'

Ned had a lot of love to give a woman. Freya appreciated that now. To the right kind of woman who could make a life here with him. Not someone like her, terrified of the isolation, the slithery things, the boredom of country life. Ned must think she was such a wimp, afraid of so much, even his old dog.

She had really tried to overcome those fears, had gone to therapy once she could afford it. But what she was most frightened of was tying her life to someone else's. Not only because she didn't want anyone to control her, but also because she had lost the only people she loved and trusted. Love meant loss, so it was better not to love. No amount of therapy had helped her with that. Yet somewhere deep in her barricaded heart, she had longed for love and an intimate connection with a man. She had cautiously let some of those barriers down for the rock musician but he had abused her trust and trashed her vulnerable heart. Never again.

There was something strong and compelling there between her and Ned. She had felt it from the get-go and was sure he had too. She couldn't put a name to it—it was more than sexual, although it was most certainly that too. But, nameless or not, it was an attraction she fought with the same strength she fought a rogue current at the beach that tried to drag her out to sea. For one inexplicably painful moment she wished she could be that fortunate woman, wrapped in the love of this good man. But it couldn't be. For with that kind of love came expectations she could never see herself fulfilling and compromises she couldn't make.

Ned got up from the table, picked up his plate of unfinished dessert. Freya did the same. He turned to head towards the kitchen and then turned back to face her. His expression was very serious, stern even.

'I don't know if there is such a thing as a

"marrying kind",' he said. 'I've gone for steady girlfriends, relationships rather than casual encounters. I always thought I'd get married some day—most people do. But I'll be thirty in September—"some day" is sneaking up on me. Wil's marriage put it all into focus. I want the kind of loving relationship Wil has with Georgia. Holding Wil's little daughter Nina made me realise how much I want children of my own.' He paused. 'So I guess you could call me the marrying kind.'

'Heading for thirty does make you think,' she said, trying to keep her face inscrutable, her voice neutral. 'Although I've got a couple of years to go.'

'My parents' marriage taught me one thing. When I do get married, it will have to be to a woman who loves life in the country as much as I do. I wouldn't put myself through what my father went through when my mother left. And I wouldn't put any child of mine through what I went through.'

Freya had the feeling there was a deeper level to the conversation. That perhaps, without his putting anything on a personal basis, a position had been stated and a reply was required.

'I understand where you're coming from. I didn't have a home of my own for a long time. I've found my place in the city—it's where I live and where I work and…and it validates me.'

He forced a laugh; it was almost painful for her to hear. 'We're entirely at cross purposes.'

She choked out the words. 'Looks like it.'

CHAPTER EIGHT

LATER THAT NIGHT, Ned awoke to a clap of thunder so loud he felt the house shake. From her dog bed in the corner of his bedroom, Molly whimpered. Forks of lightning illuminated the room as if it were midday. Rain drummed down on the roof and gushed along the gutters and down the drainpipes outside his upstairs window.

Ned switched on his bedside lamp and swung out of bed. 'It's all right, girl,' he said to his dog, leaning down to pat her. 'You're safe here.'

Molly had been frightened of storms since she was a pup. Ned felt exhilarated by them. He loved the display of nature's power. And, as a farmer in a country where the threat of drought was constant, he relished the sound of the rain filling his property's dams and the collection tanks that provided household water.

Freya had surprised him when she had confessed to a fear of storms. He understood the fear of dogs, certainly the fear of snakes, which was shared by nearly every person he knew. But storms? She seemed somehow fiercer than that.

Freya.

Ned realised it wasn't just the thunder that had woken him, or Molly's whimper. Rather it was a strong impulse that Freya needed him.

Perhaps it was a remnant from a dream, or his concern for her alone in the cottage. He had suggested she stay in the house for the night but she had—unsurprisingly—insisted on her independence in the cottage. He had escorted her to her accommodation then gone back to his immaculate hotel-style bedroom.

Lying by himself in the king-sized bed, as he'd struggled to get to sleep, he'd felt lonelier than he could ever remember feeling. He was disconcerted by Freya's insistence he was the 'marrying kind', who wasn't married. It was nearly as bad as cousin Erin's 'never a groom' remarks. He was even more disconcerted by the fact Freya didn't meet one of his bride criteria but checked so many other boxes in terms of appeal, including being beautiful, sexy, smart, and damn good company. He couldn't get her out of his mind.

He checked the illuminated clock on his nightstand. Past midnight. He needed to see if she was okay. Ned was a practical, down-to-earth kind of guy. Yet somehow he thought he could hear her calling him, although common sense told him her voice was only in his head.

Hastily, he pulled on jeans and a sweater over his pyjamas, then his boots. He reassured Molly he wouldn't be long. As he turned towards the door, the room was pitched into sudden darkness. No lamp. No glow from the clock. Just the eerie sound of electric appliances whirring down after their power source had been cut off.

Blackout.

Power failures were nothing unusual out here. A tree could have come down over power lines. Ned grabbed his phone and put it on torch mode. He needed to get downstairs and slam down the lever that would turn on the emergency, diesel-driven generator. Power would be restored to the house within minutes.

But not to the guest cottage.

Ned ran down the stairs as fast as it was

safe to do so in the darkness. He reached the emergency-power lever and activated it. Located the powerful, emergency torch. From the coat room he grabbed both his own long oil-skin wet-weather coat, and his mother's much smaller one. By the time he was out of the door, the power was back on at the house.

He hoped Freya was sleeping through it all. But that persistent, inner voice told him that might not be the case. She was frightened of storms and she was in the pitch black of a clouded night with no illumination from the moon and none of the street lighting she was used to in the city. The motion-detector lights on the outside of the house came on to light his way as he splashed down the gravel path towards the cottage.

As expected, the cottage was in complete darkness. He called her name once, twice, three times with increasing levels of urgency.

'Freya!' He banged on the door. 'Are you okay?'

He strained to hear any response from her. Nothing. If she was asleep, she might not thank him if he barged in uninvited.

Thunder struck again and the night sky lit

up with forked lightning. This time he thought he heard a muted scream from inside. Without hesitating, he pulled out the key from his pocket and opened the door.

With the wide beam of the torch, he scanned the rooms. 'Freya!'

The living area and kitchen were empty. The bed in the master bedroom had been slept in, the quilt and sheets thrown back. The other bedroom was untouched. No one in either bathroom.

Where was she?

Had she tried to get up to the house and got lost in the dark?

A flash of lightning illuminated the entire area. The utility-room door was open; a dark shape lay huddled on the tiled floor near the washing machine. Ned's heart hammered and his mouth went dry.

He aimed the beam of the torch on the dark shape. Freya. She was curled into a ball, cocooned in the knitted grey throw rug from the bed, only the purple stripe in her hair visible, a set of headphones blocking her ears. Her breath was coming in shuddering gasps, but he could tell she was trying to mumble something.

He propped the torch so it cast a pool of soft light on her, and left his hands free. 'Freya?' He gently pulled the headphones off her head. She startled into a defensive position, threw her head back, stared at him mutely with huge unfocused eyes. 'Freya, it's Ned.'

Her eyes gradually focused in the dim light. 'Ned,' she croaked.

'Come here,' he said. He shucked off his wet coat. Freya hauled herself up as he reached down to scoop her up into his arms, throw rug and all. She was wearing only a T-shirt and light cotton pyjama pants and she was trembling. He held her close, his arms wrapped tightly around her. There was another loud clap of thunder and she moaned as she burrowed closer into his chest. He held her like that for what seemed like a long time, as her trembling subsided.

'Thank you,' she mumbled against his sweater. 'S…sorry. I… I usually do better than this in a storm these days.'

'No need to apologise. I'm glad to be here.'

She gave a great, heaving sigh, still with her

face pressed to his chest. 'The thunder woke me. I didn't know where I was. I… I panicked.'

Her voice wasn't steady, as if she had to fuel it with frequent small breaths. 'I've always been frightened of storms at night. When I was little, my nanna used to take me into bed with her and calm me.'

He thought about those years when she'd likely had nobody to comfort her. 'What about when you were in care?'

'There were always other kids in the room with me who were sympathetic; they were frightened themselves more often than not. Until…until the foster home where I was placed after the incident where Wil got involved. That foster mother had me down as a troublemaker. Warned me to steer clear of her husband with my "seductive ways".'

'What? How can these people get away with that?'

'It's their word against the children's.'

Ned stifled a curse. Again, he silently thanked Wil for protecting Freya all those years ago.

Freya snuffled as she talked to him in the dark, her voice edged with raw emotion.

'There was a storm. I cried out in the night. The woman came to the room I shared with her daughter. She said I was too old to be frightened of storms at age thirteen and that I was disturbing others in the house. She dragged me out of bed and locked me in the utility room. Told me not to be such a scaredy-cat and left me there all night. Every time it stormed, I'd be put back there.'

Ned growled. Unable to find words to express his disgust and anger at such cruelty. 'So why are you in this utility room?'

'Because there wasn't enough floor space in the closet.'

The thought of her cowering in a closet as a storm raged was heart-wrenching. 'I see,' was all he could manage to choke out, while holding her even closer.

'It's the thunder and lightning that scares me, not the rain. The fear is called astraphobia, and apparently it's quite common.'

'A phobia that the cruel woman who threw you in the laundry room only made worse.'

'Quite likely,' she said. 'I… I've seen a therapist who helped me with coping strategies. Wrap up tight in something warm, and cover my head. Use noise-cancelling headphones to block the sound of the thunder—I play music through mine—then chant a mantra to make less room for fear in my mind.'

'Please come up to the house. I hate the idea of you being down here by yourself. The power has gone off and I don't know when it'll be back on. There's an emergency generator for the house and you'll have light up there at least.' Otherwise, he'd stay here with her. He would insist on it.

There was another massive thunder clap. Freya shuddered in his arms but didn't make so much as a whimper.

'I… I can't go outside in that. Please. Let me stay inside. But don't go. I… I feel better… safer with you here.' As if he would leave her.

Ned picked up the torch, led Freya out of the utility room to the living room, where he lowered her to the sofa and sat next to her, propping the torch on the coffee table. He wrapped the rug around her again and drew her close. When she got her breathing back to a more normal rhythm, he spoke. 'How did you get to be in the care of such unfeeling—some downright dangerous—people, without anyone on your side?'

With only the light of the torch he couldn't see her face to gauge her reaction to his words. She didn't reply. How could he help her if he didn't know what had caused her fears?

She opened her mouth to speak, then she sighed, as if she was too weary to keep up the blockade on her past life. 'My mother had me when she was seventeen. She'd run away from home to be with her older, drug-dealer boyfriend—my father, as it turned out. When she fell pregnant he booted her back home to my grandparents. To their tiny two-bedroom terraced cottage.'

'They took her in?' he said cautiously.

'As they'd done many times before. She was their only child. Only this time they did it on the proviso that she looked after herself while she was pregnant. That meant staying off the drugs. She complied. Nanna told me Mum wanted the baby. Wanted it to be healthy. The boyfriend stayed away. Nanna and Pop really thought she'd turned the corner. That maybe the pregnancy, though unplanned, might be the making of her.'

'But that wasn't the case?'

Her voice was gaining in strength. 'Unfortunately not. Once she'd had the baby—me—and got her figure back, the boyfriend crooked his little finger and she went running back.'

'Did she take you with her?'

'Apparently she tried to care for me. But a baby cramped his style. That's according to my grandparents. I remember Nanna telling me she worried herself sick for my safety every night I spent with my parents. One day, when I was only a few months old, my mother brought me home, said she couldn't look after me and asked my grandparents to look after me.'

Ned was horrified; her parents had had a duty to care for her. But he fought to keep his voice neutral, not judgemental. He didn't want her to clam up. 'That was probably a good thing.'

'Yes, it was. Pop could be a bit grumpy at times, but he was very caring. Nanna was wonderful in every way. A big woman with a big heart. She loved me and I loved her. For a long time, I thought she was my mother.'

'And your real mother?'

'She flitted in and out of my life. I don't really remember her. I… I don't think she ever gave me much thought. I remember overhearing my nanna saying that all that mattered to my mother was to get her drugs and be with the man who obsessed her. Of course I didn't know what that meant at the time. She was only in her early twenties when…when she and my father were both found dead of an overdose. I was five years old.' She stumbled over the words.

'Freya, I'm so sorry.' What else could he say?

'Looking back, I see how tragic it was, the… the sordid nature of both their short lives and their deaths. Back then it didn't really affect me. Nanna and Pop became my legal guardians. They were older than other kids' parents but that was okay. I grew up not knowing anything different. Abbotsford wasn't as gentrified then as it is now. I wasn't the only one in an unconventional family.'

'That must have made it easier.' He was struggling to find the right words to respond to her; he just wanted to hold her, to make amends for something he could not.

'I went to the very good local school, had friends. There wasn't a lot of money but enough. Pop worked at the brewery and Nanna cleaned houses, work that fitted with school hours so she could be there for me when I came home. I was happy, didn't question anything. Why would I?'

'So what changed?'

She paused, drew a deep breath and exhaled it. He could feel the rise and fall of her chest against his. 'You realise how difficult talking to you like this is for me? I've shared this with very few people. I prefer to put it all behind me. It was only seeing Wil in those photos that brought my past back.'

'I understand,' he said. He was straining hard against a rush of anger towards her selfish parents. But they hadn't been much more than kids themselves.

'"What changed," you say? Everything changed.'

'Everything?'

'My happy, secure little world fell apart. My grandfather died in an industrial accident. Nanna adored him, she took it hard, especially following the loss of her only daughter. On top of that, she had developed diabetes. Looking back, I don't think she really understood how to manage her condition. When I was ten, she had to have her leg amputated.'

Ned didn't try to disguise his shock. 'I'm sorry, how dreadful. How did that affect you?'

'There was no family to help. Social services stepped in. While Nanna was in hospital and rehab—not that I really understood what all that meant, just that she wasn't there—I was placed in care.'

'A foster home?'

'Kind people, actually. Then when Nanna got out of hospital, I was allowed home. But her health deteriorated. She was in and out of hospital, and I was in and out of care. Then she had to go into a nursing home, where she didn't last long. She died when I was twelve.'

'And you went into care for good?'

'Until I was eighteen. They kick you out on your own then.'

'You were still a kid. With no support.'

'Yep. Sink or swim. But you learn to toughen up.'

'And you swam. You must have to get where

you are today. Talk about overcoming disadvantage.'

Ned tried not to think how strange this was,
to be having this kind of conversation in the
dark. But perhaps Freya would not be opening up to him like this if the situation were in
any way usual.

'To be fair, it wasn't a one hundred per cent
gloomy story.'

'Tell me the sunny part of the story,' he said.
'Please.' He needed to hear that her childhood
had not been unmitigated misery—not that he
would have been able to do anything about
it. Although his brother had. Wil had helped
her. Somehow that eased some of Ned's rage
against the unfairness of Freya's early life.

The storm was still raging overhead and the
room was illuminated by a flash of lightning.
In the second it lit the space, Ned saw her
flinch, but she continued. 'In spite of all the
disruptions, I did okay at school. And I suspect
I was mature for my age. When I was fifteen,
my "potential for further study" was recognised and I was given a place in a girls-only
residential home. It was run by an enlightened
charity. They encouraged me to complete high

school. I graduated with a decent university entrance score.'

'Impressive, after such a bumpy start. How did you manage to put yourself through uni? That must have been tough.'

'There was some government assistance and my work at the café paid the rest.'

'Then you met Hugh.'

'And my luck changed, thank heaven.' Her voice was hollow. The mask of fun, quirky Freya had slipped, and he realised it was only because she was too emotionally drained to keep it up. He was hearing her unvarnished truth. 'You know the rest,' she said.

Of course, Ned didn't know the rest, Freya thought, not all of it by a long shot. There were secrets in her past she would never reveal to anyone. She was already regretting letting down her guard and revealing so much. How had she allowed it to happen when she was usually so careful to curate the story of her life? Blame it on the storm. And Ned being there to help her in her storm panic with kindness and understanding.

She prided herself on her independence but

she had never been more pleased than when she'd opened her eyes from her cocoon on the floor to see Ned. Big, strong Ned sweeping her up into his arms as if she were thistledown, holding her close, wrapping her in warmth and security. He'd murmured a litany of soothing, calming words as he held her, until the panic that had stricken her started to recede. She could not remember when she had felt so safe and cared for.

It was irrational, her fear of thunder and lightning. She had tried to desensitise herself by researching the scientific explanations of why and how they occurred, had thought she was getting on top of her fear. But this storm was especially violent and she'd been alone in unfamiliar surroundings. Now here was Ned. And she felt so much better for his presence. If it were possible for a person to physically fight thunderbolts and deflect lightning strikes to protect her, she felt Ned could do it.

'Thank you for being here,' she choked out, staying near to him on the sofa.

Pressed close to his reassuring strength, she felt she could stay like that for ever. Through the thin fabric of her T-shirt she was intensely aware of his body, of the hard muscles under the soft wool of his sweater, his thighs braced next to hers. His scent was already familiar and arousing. Desire, fierce and urgent, took hold of her. She eased back from her closeness to him just enough so she could look up at his face—his handsome face that could be stern but always kind. Her eyes were getting accustomed to the dim light of his torch and she could see concern and, thrillingly, an answering desire in his eyes. They had been moving towards this since the moment they'd met.

As she raised her face to his, he lowered his head to her. Then his mouth was on hers, firm and warm and utterly wonderful—as somehow she had known in her heart that it would be. With a little murmur of pleasure and delight she kissed him back, parting her lips to receive his tongue, meeting it with hers, tasting, exploring, possessing.

The throw rug she had grabbed from the bed fell away from her. She didn't need it, not when she had the warmth and security of Ned's arms around her. She reached up and wound her arms around his neck to bring him closer.

It was their first kiss, but somehow they seemed perfectly in sync, as if they already knew each other's wants and needs. As they kissed, the storm raged around the cottage but she was scarcely aware of it. Kissing Ned was so much more effective at distracting her than any mantra or headphones could ever be.

Their kiss grew deeper, more urgent, her breathing ragged in echo of his. 'Freya,' he moaned against her mouth.

His hands slid down her body, skimmed the side of her breasts, rested on her waist, then slid down to cup her bottom. She shuddered with pleasure at the intimacy of the touch, his hands warm and firm through the fine fabric of her pyjamas.

More.

She wanted so much more. Was this over-whelming desire a reaction to danger averted? If so, she wasn't going to fight it.

'I think I should take you up to the house, where there's light and warmth,' he said, his voice husky.

'Please. I… I've had enough of the dark.'

He lifted her up from the sofa so she stood next to him. She felt immediately bereft, so reached up to claim another kiss. He raised her up so she could wrap her legs around his waist, her face now on a level with his, their kiss deep and hungry and demanding.

Finally she came up for breath, murmured her pleasure as he kissed a pathway down her neck to the hollows of her throat. Her nipples tightened and tingled and she ached for him to touch her there.

Still holding her tight, her legs wrapped around his waist, he turned them both around. He hardly seemed aware of her weight and Freya delighted in how strong he was.

While making sure she was secure, he picked up his torch. He snagged a coat, which hadn't been there before, from where it was draped across the back of a chair.

He kissed her again, swiftly and thoroughly. 'I don't want to put you down, you feel so good right where you are.' His breathing was ragged. 'But it's still raining and you need this coat.'

Reluctantly, she unhooked her legs and slid to the ground. Solicitously, he helped her into the raincoat. It was a bit big for her, but obviously a woman's coat. Did it belong to a former girlfriend? If so, how did she feel about wearing it?

'The coat is my mother's,' he said, answering her unasked question. 'I'll grab mine from the utility room where I left it when I found you. But I'll need the torch.' His fingers brushed her cheek. 'Will you be okay here without the light? It will only be for a few seconds.'

'Yes,' she said through gritted teeth, refusing to admit that the thought terrified her.

But somehow it was okay as she could hear him moving around and, true to his word, he was back before she had time to miss him. He shrugged himself into his coat, then put the hood of hers over her head. 'You look very cute,' he said, kissing her.

She returned the favour, reaching up and putting his hood over his head. 'You look cute too.'

'I'm not sure about the cute bit, but thank you.' He planted another kiss on her mouth as her reward.

'My shoes,' she said, taking a step towards the bedroom.

'You won't need them. I'll carry you to the house. Are you ready?'

He swept her up into his arms and cradled her close. She held onto his shoulders. 'You're so…chivalrous,' she murmured. Excitement thrummed through her.

'Any time,' he said in that deep, manly voice.

He pulled open the door and they were met with a blast of wind and rain that made Freya cringe. Outside in the storm, she was exposed and vulnerable to her worst fears. If there was a clap of thunder, she would die of terror. But somehow she felt as though Ned was her shield against her fear and that it would be impossible to come to harm while she was with him.

'I'll make a run for it,' he said. 'I promise not to drop you.'

Could he really run with her in his arms? Turned out he could. She laughed with exhilaration. He laughed too. Then they were both laughing as he ran with her along the gravel path, the torchlight wavering ahead of them. She was snug in the raincoat and Ned's arms. Not for a moment did she worry he'd drop her.

As he neared the building, sensor lights switched on to guide them to the beautiful house that lay ahead as a place of refuge from the terrors of the storm. And she was safe in

the arms of this man she had known for so little time, yet wanted beyond all reason.

They were both breathless and laughing as
he carried her through the door and deposited
her in the welcoming warmth of the hallway.
'We made it,' he said.

'Your arms must be aching,' she said.

'Not at all,' he said. 'You—'

'Don't tell me, I'm lighter than a sheep.' But
she laughed as she said it.

She shrugged off her damp coat and he hung
it on a coat hook, then did the same with his
own coat. Freya stood there in just her light
pyjamas and T-shirt. She wore no underwear,
was aware that the fine fabric clung to the
curves of her hips and bottom, that the shape
of her breasts and her peaked nipples must be
clearly visible. He noticed and his eyes narrowed in appreciation. His gaze was like a caress and she ached for him to touch her.

He cupped her breasts in his hands, as he
pulled her to him again in a swift, passionate kiss. It felt so good her knees weakened
and she sagged against him. She wanted more
kisses, more caresses, more Ned, but while she
knew they were the only people in the house,

she felt self-conscious in a way she hadn't in the darkened cottage. 'Here's not the place,' he said, picking up on her feelings as only he seemed to have the ability to do.

He took her hand and led her towards the grand staircase.

'Where are we going?' she said.

'Upstairs,' he said.

She hadn't been upstairs yet. But his answer excited her. Because right now, a bedroom seemed like a very good idea.

CHAPTER NINE

FREYA PRIDED HERSELF on her independence, yet she revelled in the way Ned swooped her up in his arms to carry her up the stairs. There was absolutely no need for him to do so; she could easily get up the stairs under her own steam—her bare feet were hardly going to be injured by contact with the dense, luxurious carpet—but she thrilled to it. It wasn't so much the heroic, he-man display of strength, but the way Ned made her feel—cherished, protected, of value. It was a total turn-on. 'I could get used to this,' she murmured.

'It's my pleasure,' he said.

He slipped his hand under her T-shirt, touching her bare back. His hand was callused from hard manual work, and its roughness against the smoothness of her skin sent shivers of delight coursing through her. Freya ached to feel his skin against hers but there were too many layers of his clothing between them. She would have to remedy that.

He gently placed her on the floor of the landing. 'My bedroom or the guest bedroom?' he said. 'Before you reply I should warn you, Molly is in my bedroom.'

Freya felt some degree of empathy with the dog over their shared fear of storms, but she did not want to share a room with her, much as the idea of being in Ned's bedroom appealed. 'The guest room, please.'

'I asked Marian to get one of them ready for you in case the cottage didn't appeal,' he said.

He took her hand and led her up the hallway. 'This is the room,' he said, and opened the door. Freya got an initial impression of six-star hotel luxury—an enormous bed, a door opening to an en-suite bathroom, muted tones of grey and blue, the storm outside muted by heavy curtains. But her focus was on Ned.

'I'm at a distinct disadvantage in these skimpy clothes, while you're fully dressed,' she murmured. 'Let's even the score.'

'Gladly,' he said hoarsely as he kicked off his boots.

She pushed his navy knit sweater up from

his waist and helped him pull it over his head. It revealed a loose blue-and-white-striped shirt that wasn't exactly sartorially splendid but who cared? It wouldn't be on him for long. She fumbled with his belt and then the button fastening of his jeans. He helped her slide them down over his hips. Matching striped boxers? No. Longer pants than that.

'You've got stripy pyjamas on,' she said, bemused. Old-fashioned, long-sleeved dad pyjamas. Not that she had ever known her dad.

'Yeah. I threw my clothes on over them. Not for the first time. It's quick when I have to get up for an emergency.'

'Was I an emergency?' she asked flirtatiously.

'Yes,' he said simply. 'I was worried about you.'

Her heart seemed to flip over at the concern in his eyes. She wasn't used to that kind of thoughtfulness.

What was she doing letting things go this far when she knew there couldn't be a future with him?

She switched that inner voice off. She wanted Ned. He wanted her. That was all that was important. They were adults who knew what they were doing.

This was about tonight.

'I like your pyjamas,' she said stoutly, rising on tiptoe to kiss him, forgiving herself the fib.

'They're the kind I used to wear at boarding school. When it comes to clothes I just order replacements, the same again. Jeans, checked shirts, T-shirts. It saves time.'

'Why not?' she said. 'If you have your own look, stick to it.'

Again, he endeared himself to her. What you saw was what you got with Ned. He was straightforward and didn't pretend to be anyone other than he was. It was refreshing. She could even call it…lovable.

Slowly, she walked her fingers up his chest and started to undo the top button of his pyjama top. She narrowed her eyes. 'I think I'd prefer you in no pyjamas at all though.'

Ned was beyond thinking of anything but how much he wanted Freya. How alluring she was. How having her in his arms made his heart pound. How the prospect of having her in his bed was intoxicating. But through his excitement, an insistent thought pushed its way forward: Freya had to know what she was unleashing, and be sure it was what she wanted.

He put his hand over hers to still her unbuttoning of his shirt. 'Those pyjamas go off, you know what will happen.' His breathing was ragged and uneven.

'Yes,' she said. Her eyes gleamed with passion and anticipation.

Her answer aroused him even more; he wanted to stop talking and kiss her again. But Ned couldn't forget how vulnerable Freya was, how he'd felt when he'd seen her lying on that floor, a quivering mass of fear. He had to be responsible, even when all he wanted to do was divest her of her clothes and carry her to that bed.

'You're sure this is what you want?' he said.

'Very sure. I want *you*, Ned.' There was an edge of impatience to her voice.

He wouldn't hold back. 'I want you, too,' he said. More than she might imagine.

'Let's see if we can strip each other's pyjamas off at the same time,' she said with a mischievous laugh. She was *so* sexy. Her nipples were thrusting against her T-shirt. He ached to see her naked.

'Synchronised stripping?'

'Yes,' she said, laughing.

He lifted his hand from hers and she undid his top button. Her fingers were trembling, which told him she wasn't quite as assured as she wanted him to believe. He slid his hands under her T-shirt and went to pull it up and over her head.

'Uh, uh,' she said playfully. 'Let me get all your buttons undone first, so we're on an even playing field.'

Her teasing sent his excitement levels rocketing. He gritted his teeth and tried to sell himself on the virtues of delayed gratification.

Freya undid the buttons, one by one, her fingers tickling his chest, then pushed his shirt away. 'Oh, my. Ned, you have an amazing body,' she breathed. 'It's a crime to cover it up. Especially with those pyjamas.'

Ned didn't know why she found his pyjamas so unappealing—they were practical, did the job. But if she wanted to take them off, he had no problem with that. She splayed her hands across his chest, then ran them down to his waist. He gulped at the effect her touch had on his already aroused body.

'Your abs. Your pecs. You must work out, as well as haul sheep around, to get muscle like this.' Her voice was even huskier than usual as she stroked across his chest, exploring. When she looked up at him, her eyes were glazed, the pupils huge. 'You really are the most gorgeous man.'

'Nice of you to say so,' he managed to choke out through the waves of arousal fogging his brain.

But he'd had more than enough of talking. He slid his hands up under her T-shirt to cup her breasts. No bra. She moaned when he rolled her nipples between fingers and thumb. As he shrugged his shirt off his shoulders, he—at last—pulled her T-shirt over her head. Her breasts were small, high and round, with pink, peaked nipples. 'Perfect,' he breathed. '*You* are perfect. Beautiful Freya.'

She went to say something self-deprecating but he smothered her words with a kiss that started on her mouth, travelled down her throat, and finished on one, then the other, of her lovely breasts.

* * *

Freya wanted Ned so much she could make love with him then and there on the carpet. Or up against the wall. But she was glad when he steered her towards the bed.

He placed her down on the quilt as if she were something precious. She wouldn't have cared if he'd thrown her down.

She just wanted him.

She lay next to him on the bed, facing him on her side, as they kissed and caressed each other until kissing was no longer enough, and their remaining garments were getting in the way. Impatiently, she tugged at his pyjama pants, untied them and pushed them off him. He was well built *everywhere*.

He made the act of removing her pyjama pants into an extended caress, stroking and kissing along the length of her legs as he slid them off her. Then there were no barriers to intimate exploration, and she murmured and sighed with pleasure at his caresses from his skilled fingers. He seemed to know exactly what would please her and her arousal mounted. Within minutes, she was overwhelmed by an orgasm so powerful she screamed out his name.

When, dazed, she came back to earth, it was to see him looking into her face, a sensuous half-smile playing around his lips. 'Did you like that?' he murmured.

'I don't think you need to ask,' she said, still gasping as her heart rate returned to somewhere near normal.

Kind. Considerate. Gentlemanly. They were all qualities she'd attributed to Ned. If she had at any time earlier at the cottage assumed this would be gentle comfort sex, those thoughts had been thoroughly dispelled. Ned was outrageously virile. And she loved it.

'Now your turn,' she said, caressing him.

He moved her hand. 'No, I want to be with you.'

'Even better,' she whispered.

'Stay lying on your side,' he murmured. 'I'm so much bigger than you, I want you to be comfortable.'

'Sounds good to me,' she said, wiggling into the best position to receive him.

He moved to meet her so he was intimately

close. Then stopped. Cursed low and fluently. 'Protection. I don't have—'

'I'm on the pill,' she said breathlessly.

'I've tested clean,' he said.

'So have I.' She thrust her hips urgently towards him. 'Please, Ned,' she begged. 'I'm desperate for you. Don't make me wait any longer.'

He didn't, and she gladly welcomed him into her body. Immediately, he found her rhythm and she matched his, in perfect trust and harmony with each other's needs, so the act of making love seemed more profound than she had ever imagined it could be. She somehow felt complete, as if she had found something that had always evaded her. They came together, her cries of ecstasy mingling with his and the incessant storm that continued to rage outside the windows.

Afterwards, she drowsed in his arms and tried not to think about what came next. Because nothing had changed. They might be awesome in bed together but their lives were still at cross purposes. She couldn't be the woman he needed to live the life that had been mapped out for him. Forcing herself into a mould that didn't fit, just to please him, would only lead to disaster for both of them.

CHAPTER TEN

FREYA WOKE THE next morning to the joyous comfort of Ned's strong, warm body spooning her from behind, his arms tight around her. They'd fallen asleep like that after they'd woken at dawn and made love again. She felt deliciously content and boneless with sexual satisfaction. And happy. *So* happy. But it was a happiness she knew could only be momentary.

The rain was drumming relentlessly on the roof. Some found it a pleasant sound, but not her, as she always feared thunder and lightning might accompany it. Still, she was able to relax, as the security of Ned's embrace took the edge off her anxiety.

The noise that had awoken her came again— a scratching on the closed door accompanied by a piteous whining. This time Ned heard it too and he sat up, planting a quick kiss on her mouth as he did so.

'Molly needs to be taken outside for a bathroom stop. Trust me, at her advanced age, I don't ignore the requests, much as I would like to stay here with you.'

He swung himself out of bed and headed towards his discarded clothes. Freya caught her breath at the sight of him naked. Broad shoulders tapered to his superb butt, and long, powerfully muscled legs. Could a man look more wonderful? Desire rippled through her again. Through sleepy eyes she watched as he pulled on the pyjama pants, then his sweater, not bothering with his boots. Every movement was a play of muscle on muscle. She could watch him for ever.

No. She could not have such thoughts about Ned. This level of intimacy was frightening. She could never entertain the words *for ever.*

Ned opened the door to his dog. 'C'mon, girl. Let's get you downstairs.' He turned back to face Freya. 'Don't go anywhere. I'll be back.'

As if she could go anywhere in a hurry.

As if she wanted to.

Not yet. The weather had put paid to any further photography in the garden. In theory, she should pack up her van and head back to

Melbourne. But she wanted to spin this time out with Ned for a few more hours at least.

Freya yawned, stretched out her arms and snuggled back under the sheets, which smelled deliciously of *them*. Then pulled his pillow to her side of the bed and buried her face in it, breathing in his scent. She didn't know for how long she drowsed before Ned came back. He sat on the edge of the bed beside her and put his hand on her bare shoulder. 'Hey, are you awake?'

'Sort of.' She sat up, tugging the sheet in place to cover her breasts. Crazy really, when he'd seen every inch of her last night. And vice versa. This morning his face was shadowed with morning stubble, darker than his hair, and he looked sexy as hell.

He smoothed her hair, dishevelled from a night of lovemaking, back from her face. It was a tender gesture. 'Much as I'd like to climb back into bed with you, it's past nine and Marian is downstairs. I don't particularly want any gossip about you—about *us*—starting.'

Us? There could be no *us*.

'Me neither,' she said.

She was aware of a subtle shift in the dynamics between them, an awkwardness, a falling back from the joyous spontaneity of their passion the previous night.

He leaned towards her. 'Marian knows you moved up to this room from the guest cottage after it lost power. As far as she's concerned, I spent the night in my room. Not that I have to explain myself to the staff. But I would prefer to be discreet.'

'Me too,' she said.

His gaze was intent. 'Not that I'm ashamed of what happened between us. Far from it. But it's private and special.'

Her eyelashes flickered; she found it difficult to meet his gaze. 'For me too,' she said, her voice breaking.

'Special' was way too lacklustre a word to encompass the awesomeness of their lovemaking. Not just a joining of bodies but something so much more profound. She felt like weeping when she thought about how unlikely it was that she would ever again make love with Ned.

'Freya, this is bad timing, but I have to meet with my managers. There's some significant storm damage and the rain is playing havoc with the autumn planting.'

'I understand,' she said. 'The weather has played havoc with my photography of the garden too. Luckily I got a lot done yesterday, because I won't be able to shoot today. However, I think you—and your mum—will be happy with the results.'

He smiled that fabulous slow smile that warmed his eyes. 'I don't doubt that for a moment.'

'Thank you,' she said. 'I really enjoyed the shoot. But…what I'm trying to say is that I should head back to Melbourne.'

He sat back from her. 'About that. The creek has flooded, broken its banks in places. It's not too bad for us but further downstream the causeway is covered.'

'What do you mean?'

'There's water across the road that leads from here to the highway. It's way too dangerous for cars to cross. So you actually can't drive to Melbourne. And the weather is too wild to take the helicopter up.'

'You mean I'm trapped here?' She could

endure a couple of days in the country—but no more.

Immediately, she regretted the words as Ned's face fell. She'd hurt him. Just the first of a long line of hurts she would inflict on him and on herself if she...

If she let herself fall in love with him.

That was what the danger had been all along. *Love.* That trap was something she could not fall into. She couldn't start something she knew could not continue. There could only be that one night between them. One night she knew she would never forget.

'Trapped?' He scowled. 'Is that how you'd think of it?' She realised he was talking about more than a delay to her departure today. 'Would it be so terrible to have to stay here for a while longer? To stay with me?'

She met his gaze unflinchingly, although a cauldron of emotion was churning inside her. 'To stay today would be lovely. But...but after that, I have to get back to work. Things haven't changed, Ned. My life is in Melbourne.'

His jaw tightened. She read his reactions as they flicked across his face. Loss. Regret. Anger. 'Of course it is,' he said, tight-lipped.

He got up from the bed, frowned. 'Did last night…did it mean anything to you?' He paused, shook his head. 'Don't answer that.' He turned on his heel.

Freya jumped up from the bed, dragging the sheet with her for modesty. 'Ned. No. Don't go.' He turned back to face her. 'It meant so much. I've never… It…*you*…were amazing. You are so wonderful…in every way.'

His face gentled. 'One night wasn't enough for me, Freya. Not with you. There are ways around every problem. You live in Melbourne. We don't inhabit different planets.'

But they might as well do. It wasn't just the physical distance from Five and a Half Mile Creek to Melbourne. It was the difference in their life goals. Differences that were insurmountable, as far as she could see.

'True,' she said. 'We…uh…we need to talk it through.'

'Being *trapped* here might be a good time to do so,' he said. 'I'll get back up to the house as soon as I can.'

'Good idea,' she said, trying to keep the rising panic from her voice. She hated confrontation.

He took a step towards her. 'I can't tell you how sexy you look in that sheet.'

'Er…thank you,' she murmured, clutching it close.

He kissed her, a short, sweet claiming of her mouth she was unable to resist returning with a little gasp of pleasure.

But already it felt like a kiss between strangers.

Ned was later back to the house than he had anticipated. Thankfully the rain had ceased but there was extensive storm damage. Trees and fences were down, and the men were out on motorbikes checking for further damage. They might not know for days about the furthest reaches of the property. That would mean having to take up the helicopter now the weather had started to clear, this time to survey what had been destroyed rather than to do a scenic tour. Nothing was as usual. The roof had come off a feed shed. The horses were spooked. As Freya had been last night.

It turned out she spooked easily.

He wasn't thinking about her reaction to the storm though. It was her reaction to him this morning that had his gut churning. He had a horrible suspicion she intended to bolt and that would be the last he ever saw of her. She'd told him she wasn't one for long-term relationships. That could translate to *no* relationships. He should have listened to her. But would that have stopped him last night from carrying her up the stairs to the bedroom? The answer was a resounding *no*.

Her purple van parked in the driveway confirmed his suspicion. Freya was loading her equipment through the open back doors. She was dressed in the black jeans and black tunic she'd been wearing the first time he'd seen her. There was no floating scarf—but that didn't mean she wasn't flying away from him.

'Ned,' she said as he approached. 'You've been a while. Marian has saved your lunch for you.'

He shouldn't have given her time to think. But he had to lead his team inspecting the property. As always, Five and a Half Mile Creek came first.

But at what cost?

Was that the real reason he'd been 'never a groom'?

'The damage is bad, but nothing that can't be mended.'

'That's good to hear.'

He looked pointedly at her van. 'Packing up?'

'It...er...seemed a good idea to get my things from the cottage while there's a break in the rain.'

'It looks like you're packing up to go,' he said.

'It...it doesn't hurt to be prepared for when the road is open again.'

'True.'

An uncomfortable silence fell between them. Freya was the first to break it. 'Ned, about that talk. Should we have it now? Somewhere private?'

He was going to suggest the guest cottage, but then thought she would probably want to spend as little time as possible there after her traumatic experience. 'How about my study?'

'Okay.' She bit on her lower lip. Not a good sign.

Ned sat in the leather office chair in his study and swivelled it around to face her. She was sitting in his favourite easy chair. He would rather he was the one in that big chair and that he was pulling her down onto his knee. But the vibe she was giving off let him know that wasn't going to happen. She sat on the edge of the chair, her legs primly together. It felt uncomfortably like an interview—one where he had the distinct feeling he wasn't going to get the job.

'I love this room,' she said, looking around her.

'Me too,' he said. 'But then we both know that.'

'No idle chit-chat, then?' she said with a hint of her lovely smile.

'There are more important things to talk about. Like how we can continue to see each other. I… I don't want to let you go, Freya.'

Damn. He didn't want to stumble over these words, they were too important. He also didn't want to make too big a deal of it. He wasn't talking binding vows here, just making it clear he wanted to see her again. To take her to bed again.

Her eyes were very wide in her pale face. 'I don't want to let you go either, Ned.' Unfortunately the way she said it made him know her words would be followed by a *but*. 'But it can't work between us.'

'The distance is not insurmountable.'

'So you visit me in Melbourne, I visit you here,' she said. 'We date long distance.'

'Sounds like a plan.'

'And then what?'

'You tell me.'

'We hit a brick wall when it comes to a future together.' She leaned forward in her chair, grasped both hands together. 'We've had this conversation before. Cross purposes, remember? Completely different lives. Different plans for the future.'

'That was before last night.'

'Yes,' she said, her voice sad, her eyes not meeting his. 'That...that makes it so much more difficult.'

'More difficult for you to end things between us before they've even started?'

She nodded.

'Why?' He got up from his chair. Paced the distance of his desk and back. 'How can you just walk away? Last night...was something extraordinary.'

She got up to face him, a stubborn tilt to her

chin. 'Because it's better I do so now rather than further down the track when it would hurt a whole lot more. Hurt both of us.'

'Don't I have some say in that?'

'You already have had a say,' she said. 'You've stated what you want in a woman— and it isn't me. I can't be the woman you *need* for your life here. The sooner I'm out of your life, the sooner you can forget me and move on.'

'I don't want to forget you.'

'It's best that you do. We're great in bed—'

He groaned. 'At last she says something I can agree with.'

'But that won't be enough. Not if we're incompatible out of the bedroom.' She drew a deep breath. 'You're the marrying kind, remember? I'm not. I don't want to get married or live with a man. I don't want to cede any part of my life into another person's control. For too many years I had people making decision about how I lived my life that weren't always in my best interest.'

'Doesn't it depend on the man? There has to be an element of trust, surely.'

'I don't trust easily,' she said, her mouth set in a stubborn line.

'Because you've encountered too many untrustworthy men.'

'Starting with my father. Followed by some truly scary foster fathers. Then there are the controlling types. It's amazing how many of *them* want to be foster parents. Even Pop, who I loved, kept Nanna under his thumb. When he said "jump", you asked how high on the way up. Nanna was too busy looking after him— and then me—to look after herself.'

'You're lumping all men into the one category. There are plenty of good men around.'

Her face softened. She reached out just long enough to touch his cheek before she dropped her hand again. 'Including you. You're one of the good guys. Someone I could perhaps learn to trust over time. If circumstances were different.'

'Yet you don't intend to give me the chance.'

'You've also told me you want kids, right?'

'Yes. More than one. I didn't like being an only child.'

'You should know that I have never wanted to have children. I don't know that I could be a good mother, not after the upbringing I had without one of my own. Not only that, I saw too many unwanted children in my time in state care. I couldn't bear the thought of a child of mine ever ending up one of them.'

'The father might have something to say about that,' he said gruffly.

'There's something else.' Her mouth twisted. She looked up. 'It isn't just that I don't *want* to have children. I might not be *able* to have them.'

'What do you mean?'

She took a deep breath. 'I have a condition called polycystic ovarian syndrome. It's a hormonal imbalance. I take the pill to help alleviate the symptoms. My doctor tells me I might need fertility treatment if I wanted to get pregnant.'

'But you *could* get pregnant?'

'Possibly.'

'That wouldn't bother me,' he said. 'The trying, I mean.'

'It would. If you really want a family. In the future, I mean. You…you need to put me in the too-hard basket, Ned,' she said, her voice wobbling.

'You realise we're talking about the road-blocks to a future together?' he said with a puzzled frown. 'When we hardly know each other. It's…bewildering.'

'I know,' she said. 'It's kind of bizarre. I… I felt some kind of connection from the word go.'

'Me too.' He pulled her into his arms and she didn't resist. He held her close. 'I hear everything you're saying. You're right. Of course you're right. We have nothing in common.' Not one match on his wife wish-list. Yet last night, with her naked and passionate in his arms, that had seemed irrelevant. 'But I still don't want to let you go.'

She pulled away from him, and looked up at him, still within the circle of his arms. 'Would you leave Five and a Half Mile Creek for me?' She put up her hand in a halt sign. 'Don't answer that question. It's purely theoretical.'

'Freya,' he said brokenly. 'I—'

Did it always come down to that? He could have Five and a Half Mile Creek, or he could have love? Not that he was talking *love* with Freya.

'We would only end up resenting each other,'

she said. 'So let me climb into that too-hard basket where I belong, and let me drive back to Melbourne.'

'You'll go no matter what I say, won't you?'

She nodded. 'It's how it has to be. For both our sakes.'

Ned held her close again and for a long moment they stood silent. He wanted to protect her, but she didn't want to be protected. He wanted to make love to her again; she had no such interest. For her, last night had been a one-night stand. He'd be wise to think about it as that too.

'The causeway is clear, the road open,' he said. He'd known that for a couple of hours; he'd been checking the emergency services for news of further flooding, hadn't wanted to tell her, so as to spin out her time here.

'I know. I've been checking the traffic app.'

'The weather could still be dangerous.'

'Sunshine on its way, according to the radio.'

Not for him, he thought. Not without Freya in his life.

'This is unendurable,' he said.

'For now.' Her voice was muffled as her face was pressed against his chest and, he thought, from the effort of pushing back against tears. He was enduring the same struggle himself. 'When…when you're settled with your country-loving wife and a brood of kids you won't even give me a thought.'

His wife wish-list had been a stupid idea. He saw that now. Because it didn't take into account the possibility of falling for a woman who was wildly unsuitable and yet who had, last night, made him happier than he could ever have imagined he would feel. He would have to rethink everything.

He cleared his throat. 'And when you're back enjoying the buzz of the city, you'll look back and shudder at the thought of the…the slithery things.'

He'd been going to say *the country guy who wasn't exciting enough for you* but that sounded maudlin and self-pitying and probably not true. It was circumstances rather than the people they were which made this— *them*—impossible. Because he did want kids. Badly. The feelings when he'd held baby Nina at her father's wedding had been powerful and from the heart. And giving up Five and a Half

Mile Creek would be like giving up part of his soul.

She pulled away from him. Swiped at her eyes with the backs of her hands. 'I should leave sooner rather than later.'

'Yeah. Best to make a clean break. I'll head on back down to…to check on the horses.' And to gain comfort from the unconditional affection of his equine friends. Animals were so much more reliable than people.

'When you get back, I'll be gone,' she said.

His heart sank to the level of his boots at the thought of her absence. No more purple in his life. 'And after that?'

Her eyes flickered nervously. 'Perhaps, given time, we…we could salvage a friendship from this. If your mother likes the garden shoot, perhaps I could come back in spring.'

'Yeah. Perhaps.' He knew his words sounded hollow, but then so did hers.

That wouldn't happen. He wouldn't hire her again. How could he be 'just friends' with her after what they'd shared?

It was only sex, he told himself.

But he knew what had passed between them was so much more than that.

He could not endure watching her little purple van carry on down the driveway, taking her out of his life. 'Take care,' he said as he turned on his heel and walked away without looking back.

CHAPTER ELEVEN

Two months later

NED HAD HEARD from Freya three times in the last eight weeks. The first time had been three days after she'd left, when she'd sent the images from the garden shoot via an app capable of transmitting high-resolution images. Every photo had, of course, been a work of art. The file had been accompanied by a brief, impersonal email saying she hoped he would be pleased with the shoot. He had replied in kind, aching to say how much he missed her, knowing it would be inappropriate.

Her next communication had been two days after that. She'd sent an e-card, produced by her. It had been designed around the image of his hand putting his lucky horseshoe to rights, taken on the day of her first shoot in this very room, and included the words *Thank you, Ned*.

It was, as she'd said at the time, a 'cute' image and she'd turned it into a clever design. She was a very talented artist.

Freya had sent the card on a Sunday evening, perhaps when she was alone, possibly having regrets. He'd hoped so, anyway. He'd been alone too and, foolish guy, had immediately replied. He'd suggested they catch up in Melbourne, some time soon. She had tortured him by taking a day to reply, only to dash his hopes with a note saying it was too soon, she wasn't ready. Since then, nothing.

He missed her. Even though she'd only spent a few days here in total, she had made such an impact on his life. Every day, thoughts of her had drifted into his mind. He worked all hours, galloped his horses, pounded out reps in his home gym, swam laps in the enclosed heated pool. But nothing stopped those images of her from taunting him. Freya had inveigled her way into his thoughts along with a truckload of *what ifs* and *if onlys* that he wasn't used to entertaining.

Recently those thoughts had been of the same disturbing kind he'd felt on the night he'd rescued her from the cottage during the storm. That she needed him, that she was calling for him.

Wishful thinking, mate.

He was just looking for an excuse to see her.

Still, the idea wouldn't let go that she needed him. Though in reality it was more likely he needed her.

He scrolled down to the emails he'd sent last Friday—not to Freya, but to his family friend Hugh Tran, her boss.

Hi Hugh

I'll be in Melbourne next week. Would like to discuss enlarging and printing some images of the garden shoot Freya did for Mum. Will you be around on the Wednesday?

Ned

Hi Ned

Yes to Wednesday, it would be great to see you. It's Freya you will need to see re the garden pics. I'll make sure she'll be at the studio on Wednesday morning.

Hugh

Hi Hugh
Excellent. See you Wednesday morning around ten.
Ned

Ned shut down his computer. It was Monday night. There was too much to do here to waste the time it would take to drive to Melbourne. He'd fly the helicopter down tomorrow, land it at the helipad in the family home in Toorak, then spend the night in his penthouse apartment nearby. On Wednesday he'd make his way to Hugh's Richmond studio in the car he kept at the apartment for his and Wil's use. He had no other appointments. There was only one reason for a trip to Melbourne.

To see Freya.

Traffic coming into Richmond on this wintry morning had been hell and Ned was glad he'd left Toorak in plenty of time to get to Hugh's studio.

He'd actually been early, and spent ten minutes finding the café he thought might be the one Freya had worked in, and where she'd first met Hugh. As he sat in his car and drank his takeaway coffee he marvelled, not for the first time, at how incredible it was that Freya, who Wil had known as Tegan, had been so close to the family for all that time, and at the coincidence that had brought her to Five and a Half Mile Creek—and him.

The studio was a low, squat building painted in bright multicoloured blocks, and shared the narrow street with other converted warehouses, auto workshops and a scattering of terrace houses in varying stages of renovation. There was an abundance of graffiti on fences and walls. Ned couldn't understand how anyone could find such vandalism exciting—let alone call it art. He wasn't happy about leaving his new-model, luxury sports car parked on these mean streets. Then he smiled to himself, the thought reminding him how reluctant Freya had been to leave her equipment in her van parked on his driveway. This was her territory.

Ned had to concede there was an energy and excitement to the place. He'd forgotten—or made himself forget—how much he'd once enjoyed that aspect of city living. He wasn't yet thirty, yet he viewed city life like some rigid, over-critical middle-aged man. How had he let that happen? Why had he allowed his world to shrink to the perimeters of his own land?

The interior of Hugh's premises was spartan, with a number of studios ranging from the cavernous to the small that only came to life when they were dressed for a shoot. The small reception area was decorated simply with a series of blow-up photographs in black and white. Ned wondered if any of them were Freya's.

Hugh greeted him effusively. Ned towered over Vietnamese-Australian Hugh, but the older man's hug was strong and as affectionate as ever. Ned had always liked him; as a child he'd called him 'Uncle Hugh'.

'I didn't tell Freya you were coming,' Hugh said, when the hugs and extended greetings were over.

Ned wondered why. Because she would be elsewhere if she was aware of his visit? How much did Hugh know—or guess—about what had happened between his protégée and his old friend's son at Five and a Half Mile Creek?

'Okay,' Ned said, fighting a battle with himself to appear unperturbed. 'I guess she doesn't need notice and can readily access the photos I want to discuss with her.' Which could as easily be done over the Internet, as Hugh would well know.

'Sure she can,' Hugh said. 'She's in Studio Two.'

'I remember where that is,' Ned said. He couldn't wait a minute longer to see Freya. Eight weeks was a long time—would she have forgotten him?

He headed in the direction of the studio but Hugh stopped him with a restraining hand on his arm. 'Do you remember when you were living in Brunswick with us, and you found that injured magpie?'

'Vaguely, yes.' It had been a long time ago and Ned had helped many injured birds and animals since. 'I got it flying again.'

'You did. Just keep in mind how good you are at helping birds with broken wings.'

Ned wondered what on earth Hugh could mean. But he understood as soon as he saw Freya.

The studio door was open and she didn't appear to hear him coming in. Dressed in her usual black, she was sitting at a desk, working simultaneously on three computer screens, head down, fingers flying, intent on her work.

'Freya,' he said as he got closer.

She froze. Swivelled around on her chair. Stood up. One hand clutched at the back of the chair, the other at her heart. *'Ned.'*

The colour drained from her face, her eyes widened, then started to roll upwards as she seemed to fold in on herself.

Ned caught her before she fell, eyes closed, against him. He held her tight. Terror gripped him with icy claws. 'Freya. *Freya.*'

She was breathing, but he picked her up and laid her on the floor on her side in the recovery position. He opened her mouth to check for any obstruction, didn't find anything. He had his phone out ready to call for an ambulance when she opened her eyes. Gradually they came into focus. 'Ned?'

Thank heaven.

'I'm here, Freya.'

'Wh…what happened?'

'You collapsed. I think you fainted. I'm calling an ambulance.' He started to stab in the emergency number on his phone.

'*No*. Don't do that.' She struggled to get up and he helped her first into a sitting position on the floor and then back into her chair.

'But you're ill. I'm worried—'

'I'm not ill, Ned. I… I'm pregnant.'

What was Ned doing here?

One part of Freya rejoiced as she scanned his well-remembered features; the other cringed from the severity of his frown.

'*Pregnant?*'

'I'm sorry I didn't tell you.'

'You mean—?'

She nodded. 'The baby is yours.'

Even through her feelings of shock, lingering nausea and guilt, Freya was stunned by the expressions that flitted across Ned's face. Initial disbelief, suspicion and astonishment were replaced by a dawning wonder.

'But how?'

'The…er…usual way. Um…three times that night, if you recall.' She felt herself blush, which was crazy after all they'd bared to each other during their time together.

'But you told me you couldn't get pregnant.'

She shook her head. 'I said I'd been told I

could have trouble falling pregnant. Significant difference.'

'And you were on the pill.'

'I'm on a very low-dose pill and I have to confess I…er…forgot to take it that…that last morning. I didn't worry when I realised I'd skipped it, as I was convinced I couldn't ever get pregnant. The chances were so low for me to conceive.'

He seemed to be reeling at her news. 'You don't look pregnant.'

'I'm only eight weeks, not showing yet.' She patted her still-flat tummy.

'So…it's somewhat of a miracle?'

'In a way, yes. I got the shock of my life when the doctor told me I was pregnant. I thought I had a gastric flu. That was actually the first time I fainted. You know I never wanted to have children. But then…then I was overwhelmed by this…this joy bubbling through me, sudden and totally unexpected. It's knocked my life off course, but I really want this baby.'

'Why didn't you tell me? Did you *ever* intend to tell me?'

She couldn't meet his gaze. 'I… I was scared to tell you.'

'*Scared?*' The word exploded from him. 'Scared of *me*?'

She felt at a disadvantage sitting down but as she stood up she felt a little dizzy. Ned was there like a shot to support her. *Ned.* She couldn't believe he was here.

She shook her head. 'No. Never scared of you.'

'Well, you did faint at the sight of me,' he said wryly.

'It was a shock to turn around and see you there. Why didn't you warn me you were coming?'

'Would you have been here if you'd known?'

'Yes. No. I don't know. What I mean is I was scared of your reaction. That you might think I… I'd got pregnant on purpose.'

'As you made it very clear you didn't want to have children, I doubt I would have jumped to that conclusion.'

'But I could have been scamming you. I couldn't bear it if you thought that.'

'As if I'd think you were out to scam me,' he scoffed.

'You did think it. You're very wealthy. That night at dinner, when I told you who I was, I saw the look on your face when you thought I might have come to Five and a Half Mile Creek to stake some claim on Wil. Your disgust when you suspected I was a…a gold-digger. Maybe even a blackmailer. I was terrified to tell you I was pregnant in case…in case you thought I would make demands on you.'

'Were you?' For the first time she saw that wonderful Ned smile. Her heart had felt frozen since she'd left him. Now his smile made it start to thaw.

'Yes.'

'Of course I expect you to make demands on me,' he said.

She stilled. 'Wh…what do you mean, demands? I can support myself and the baby. I won't ask—'

'I expect you to demand that I marry you,' he said, his smile splitting into a big grin.

Freya was so shocked that for a long moment she couldn't find her voice but she couldn't help a shaky smile in return. Why did just being near Ned make her feel so much better?

'That's lovely of you, Ned, but I'm not asking you to marry me.'

'So I'll ask you to marry me,' he said immediately. 'Shall I go down on bended knee? Or will a standing proposal work?'

'Neither. I don't expect you to marry me, although I do appreciate the gesture.'

His frown banished every trace of his smile. 'You don't get it, Freya. This isn't a *gesture*. I'm not just doing the gentlemanly thing here. I want you to marry me. You're pregnant with our baby.'

'And you want to do the "right thing".'

'The right thing, yes. For you, for me, for the baby. Hudson children are not born outside…outside wedlock.' He stumbled on the old-fashioned word.

'But we hardly know each other.'

'We know enough.' He had a stubborn set to his jaw.

'All those barriers that stopped us from dating, let alone getting married, are still there.'

'Except one—that you didn't plan to have children and I did. I'm over the moon about this, Freya. I haven't stopped thinking about you since you left. I've missed you. There's something there between us, something… almost inexplicable. Can you deny it?'

Slowly, she shook her head. 'No. I can't deny it. I felt it. And… I missed you too.' The night she'd sent that e-card she'd thought she would die of the yearning for him. 'But all those other reasons for keeping us apart are still there.'

There was a loud knock on the door, followed by Hugh.

Her boss looked from Ned to her and back to Ned. 'So she's told you?'

'Yes,' said Ned, not taking his eyes off her. 'I'm shocked, but delighted I'm going to be a dad.'

'But has she told you the rest?'

Freya glared at Hugh, willing him to stay quiet.

'What do you mean "the rest"?' Ned asked.

'That her doctor has told her she needs to take it easy for the first few months of her pregnancy. That she shouldn't be working. Certainly not hauling around heavy equipment or travelling around on shoots. I've put her on light duties.' He indicated the desk where she was working on editing images and designing brochures for a client. 'But what I really want to do is sign her off on leave.'

'She should come to Five and a Half Mile Creek where she can relax and I can take care of her,' Ned said immediately.

'Those are exactly my thoughts, too,' said Hugh, beaming.

'And what about *my* thoughts?' Freya asked.

'I suspect you'll want to do what you think is best for the baby,' said Ned. 'Sometimes you have to accept a helping hand when it's offered, Freya. Will you come back to Five and a Half Mile Creek with me?'

'You know I don't need rescuing, right?'

'I'm aware of that.'

'Okay,' she said. 'I'll do it.' Hugh smiled and nodded in approval before quietly slipping out of the door. Another burst of joy had shimmered through her as soon as she'd agreed. It must be hormones; there was no other explanation. 'On the condition we don't tell anyone I'm pregnant, it's early days yet.'

'Good. I accept that condition. But I have one of my own.'

'Yes?' she said.

'I don't intend to stop asking you to marry me.'

'And I won't stop saying no,' she said.

'Game on,' he said.

That brought a hysterical laugh from her. In no way was this a *game*.

Ned waited for Freya in the living room of her tiny, one-bedroomed apartment above a small Korean supermarket, just a few streets away from Hugh's studio. She was in the bedroom packing what she needed for her trip back to Five and a Half Mile Creek with him. Her photography equipment was already stashed in his car. She didn't go anywhere without that, she'd said.

The apartment was what he might have expected from creative Freya—warm and vibrant, decorated in an eclectic manner. Silk scarves in a myriad jewel colours were draped over worn leather chairs; exotic wall hangings caught the eye; Moroccan lamps, fat scented candles, an orchid in full bloom, all were artfully placed to make the best of the small space, highlighted of course with splashes of purple. Shabby but chic oriental carpets softened the dark floorboards. It could have looked chaotic but it didn't. The room was intensely personal, yet immediately welcoming.

Through an open window that faced the street wafted spicy scents, the sound of a blues guitar from the bistro next door, and bursts of laughter from a group of students waiting at a bus stop. She would never feel alone here, he thought. Or hungry—he'd counted six restaurants and cafés with cuisines from around the world on her block alone. As well as several of the coffee shops she liked so much.

He thought he remembered going to see bands at the big pub on the next corner. One of his friends at uni had lived somewhere nearby in a slovenly student flat, with a shifting population, that had been quite a shock to the boy from a Toorak mansion and the splendours of Five and a Half Mile Creek. And he'd loved it.

Freya came out of the bedroom carrying a suitcase that he immediately took from her. Over her shoulder he could see her bedroom was decorated in the same eclectic style, an old brass bed piled with colourful cushions.

'I like your apartment,' he said.

'I love it,' she said. 'Small space, big mortgage, but it brings me joy. The one thing I wanted above all when I got out of care was my own home that no one could kick me out of. I started to save for a deposit the day I started working.'

Ned had grown up with two luxurious homes and the security of knowing he belonged there. Freya had had no such assurance. He admired her for making her own, secure home through her own efforts.

'Well done,' he said.

He looked around him. Charming as it was, it was a single person's space. Not much room for a baby. He knew Nina came with a whole lot of paraphernalia deemed essential by her parents.

'There's an enclosed sunroom off my bedroom, which will be the nursery, in case you're wondering,' Freya said as she headed towards the door.

As she led Ned down the stairs to the street Freya remembered her orchid. She didn't know for how long she'd be away but it would be at least a week, she imagined. The plant might die in that time. 'I need to pop in to my neighbours in the supermarket and ask them to water my potted plant while I'm away,' she said.

He raised his eyebrows. 'You trust them with a key?'

'Of course,' she said. 'All the people living nearby have each other's keys in case of emergencies.'

'Yet you wanted to lock your car in the country?'

'That's different—that's protection from strangers. These are my neighbours. We're quite the little community here and look out for each other. We know the people in the other shops and restaurants as well. I feel really safe. It's another reason I like living here.'

'I see,' he said. As she followed him to where he was parked, she wondered if he actually did. And yet it struck her how at home he seemed on these city streets in black jeans and an edgy deep charcoal coat. More than a few women's heads turned in his direction— something she found disconcerting.

She hadn't quite got her head around the situation she'd found herself in—agreeing to go back to his home with the father of her baby.

But she was still feeling vaguely nauseous and light-headed and didn't want to get into heavy discussions about expectations—and certainly not about marriage.

Nevertheless, she tried to keep up some kind of conversation with Ned as she sat beside him in his car—a fabulously expensive European model he'd mentioned he kept garaged in Melbourne to be used when he was in town. What was that saying? *The rich are different*. Every moment with Ned made her aware of the truth of it. He didn't even seem aware that ordinary mortals couldn't dream of such an extravagance.

A fifteen-minute drive from Richmond took them into a completely different world—affluent, elite Toorak, one of the most expensive suburbs in Australia. Its gracious streets were home to socialites, celebrities, and the seriously wealthy. Toorak hosted consulates from major-player countries like Britain, the USA and China. And the Hudson family from Five and a Half Mile Creek.

Ned explained he needed to pick up his stuff from his apartment where he had spent the previous night. Then he would drive to the nearby family mansion to access the helipad near the tennis court and swimming pool. They would leave from there via helicopter, the same one Ned had taken her up in on her first visit to his home.

Ned's city home was the penthouse of an elegant Georgian-inspired apartment block. An elevator whisked them straight up from the underground garage to the entrance hallway of his apartment.

'You call this an apartment?' she said, looking around her. 'It's the size of a large house.'

'I'm used to wide open spaces,' he said. She wasn't sure if he was joking or not.

'You must have felt very cramped in my little space.'

He would have felt as if he was slumming it. Again, she felt slammed by the differences in their social standing—although she told herself she was his equal in every other way.

'For a big guy like me it's a touch on the small side. But it's warm and welcoming and it expresses your personality perfectly. Your apartment must be a really fun place to live. If we'd had time I would have liked to follow the strains of that jazz guitar down to the bis-

tro and settle us in to listen with a coffee and
a baguette. It reminded me of the time when
I used to have a lot of fun in Melbourne before—'

'Before what?'

'Before I had to step up to my responsibili-
ties,' he said shortly, not inviting further dis-
cussion.

The house-sized apartment was splendid,
decorated in tones of grey and silver with
ebony woodwork. Opulent but masculine.
Veering on the sterile, Freya thought, but of
course didn't say. It seemed a lonely place. Although the heating was on, she shivered.

'Did your mother design the interiors?' Her
voice actually echoed in the emptiness.

'Of course. I got her to refurbish it a few
years ago.'

'But it must have been quite new then.
Why—?'

'Because I wanted to eradicate all trace of
that woman I told you about. She spent a lot
of time here.'

'She really hurt you,' Freya said slowly.

'I got over it,' he said curtly.

'But what—?'

'I was spending way too much time with her here in Melbourne, neglecting my duties at Five and a Half Mile Creek. When my mother was diagnosed with cancer, my father had to beg me to come back. Beg his own son, the heir to the property. My girlfriend didn't care enough about me or my family to even consider coming back with me. That's it. I don't want to discuss it any further.'

'I see,' said Freya. It explained a lot about why Mr Eligible was still single, why he buried himself out there at the property with little chance of connecting with anyone.

'Do you want something to eat while we're here?' he said. 'The kitchen is stocked. I have a housekeeper I notify when Wil or I are coming to Melbourne.'

Freya put her hand to her throat. 'No, thank you. I don't trust myself not to feel nauseous on the helicopter ride.' She patted her handbag. 'I've got some dry crackers here.'

'If you're sure, then we'll get moving. I'll get my bag from my bedroom.'

She followed him down the hallway, curious to see more of his home away from home. His bedroom was palatial, dominated by an enormous, super-king-sized bed. His mono-grammed leather overnight bag was already packed.

As he picked it up Freya tried not to look at the bed. He turned and his gaze connected with hers. He was also trying not to look at the bed. Tension hummed between them. Her nipples hardened.

She still wanted him.

He was the father of her baby. But to give into the urge to put her arms around his neck, kiss him and tumble together onto the bed would be foolish beyond belief.

She was pregnant, but nothing else had changed between them. The contrasts between the way they each lived in Melbourne only re-inforced their innate incompatibility.

CHAPTER TWELVE

DESPITE HIS STATEMENT of intent, once back at Five and a Half Mile Creek, Ned did not bombard Freya with proposals of marriage, for which she was profoundly grateful. To marry Ned because she was pregnant—when marriage had otherwise been so completely off the cards—was a monumental decision. To choose not to marry and somehow share the custody and upbringing of their child was equally monumental.

Whatever her decision, her life had been turned completely upside down by her unplanned pregnancy. Because, despite her long-held opinion that she never wanted to have children, she was happy at a deep, soul level at the prospect of being a mother. Already she felt a fierce love for her baby.

Ned had done everything he could to make her enforced rest comfortable. Not in the cottage—she couldn't bear to go back there—

but in the luxurious guest room they had shared. He'd made no demands on her, rather behaved like a considerate friend. The attraction between them still hummed along, but it was as if they had—by mutual consent—put it on hold until she felt better.

She'd been shocked—and more than a little scared—of how exhausted she'd been and how much sleep she'd needed. Even now, after five days here, she was only halfway back to her old energy levels. During her days of bed rest, she'd thought a lot about what Ned had said about needing 'to accept a helping hand'. Was to accept help in the form of a marriage proposal the right thing to do?

She'd spent the last ten years fiercely defending her independence and found it difficult to cede even a scrap of it for fear of losing control of her life. Now she was responsible for another life growing inside her. She still couldn't quite get her head around the idea. Perhaps she wouldn't until her baby was born and they met face to face. But her baby would grow into a child, then a teenager, then an adult. The decisions she made now would affect his or her entire life. It was up to her to make the right choices to the best of her ability.

After breakfast, she headed down to the horse yards. During her explorations of the property, beyond the bounds of the house and garden, she always took her camera with her and had found a new delight in photographing Ned's horses.

Today she'd asked Ned if she could take photos of him on horseback and he'd agreed. He waved a greeting as he led Hero, his black thoroughbred gelding, out of his stable and towards the competition-sized sand arena. Freya had to turn a gasp of admiration into a pretend cough. The gasp wasn't for Hero—though he was a superb-looking horse—it was for Ned. He wore perfectly fitted riding breeches that outlined every muscle, a tight-fitting polo shirt that emphasised his broad shoulders and powerful torso, and high black boots that were quite the sexiest thing she'd ever seen him wear. She felt quite light-headed, not with low blood pressure but with a heady mix of admiration and desire.

She watched him mount his horse and take Hero through a series of warm-up exercises.

On horseback Ned was magnificent. A highly skilled athlete. This was Ned in his true environment. He'd fitted in in Toorak too, but no wonder he preferred it here.

He was training Hero for polocrosse, a game Freya had never heard of, but which he'd explained was a combination of polo and lacrosse, and sometimes referred to as rugby on horseback. He took Hero through a series of quick changes of direction.

Freya marvelled at the rapport and respect between rider and horse—each a superb specimen of their species. No use of cruel whips or spurs for Ned, just commands transmitted through his hands and legs, he'd explained. Love too. He obviously loved his horse as he loved his dog.

As he would love his child.

She pushed that thought quickly to the back of her mind, although she knew it wouldn't stay there for long. And certainly didn't entertain the thought of what it might be like if Ned loved *her.*

She set up her camera on a high tripod. On his advice, she stayed outside the railings that surrounded the arena. He'd explained that, while his horses were very well trained, and bred for temperament as well as skill, horses were flighty creatures and he wanted her safe at all times.

She signalled to Ned that she was about to start shooting. He cantered Hero towards her, in a tightly controlled pattern of turns. In her heart, she knew her shots of him would be good. Better than good. The combination of man and horse was awesome. She was loving this.

No one could be more ignorant about horses than her. It had taken her by surprise at how fascinated she had become by them, since she'd been back at Five and a Half Mile Creek. How she'd found a new interest in photographing horses. She was even growing to appreciate the scent of a clean, healthy horse.

Ned dismounted and swung himself over the fence. Freya hadn't fainted since that day in Hugh's studio when Ned had come to find her, but the sight of him, muscles defined, a slight sheen of sweat, his smile of intense satisfaction with his ride, almost made her swoon.

Her feelings towards him were all over the place, rocketing from elation in his company,

plummeting to despair when she believed he
was only interested in her because she was
carrying his child. It was safer to keep her
distance, to suppress that desire. There were
enough hormones surging though her already,
disrupting what should be a rational process
of decision-making.

He fitted in here like the person he was—
someone born to this level of wealth and pres-
tige. Whereas she felt she would never fit.
They might as well live on different planets.
Yet her child would be born to this as Ned
had been. How could she deny her child their
birthright?

Back in Melbourne at his palatial penthouse,
she had been aware that Ned wasn't just from
the country, he belonged in the city too. But
she and he came from two very different Mel-
bournes. She had never been more aware of
the differences in status and background between them. Much as she fought those feelings
of insecurity, they continued to creep through,
not a good combination with those fluctuat-
ing hormones.

Now, she resisted the urge to throw her arms
around his neck and press her body to his;

rather she kept her distance. 'Brilliant,' she said. 'I'm in awe of both you and Hero.'

Ned patted his horse on its sweat-flicked neck. 'He's a well-mannered, honest horse and a joy to ride.' Freya risked a cautious pat too. Ned handed the reins to the stablehand to take Hero back to the state-of-the-art stables and wash him down after his workout.

I'd like to wash Ned down after his ride.

Freya flushed as she fought the image of gorgeous Ned naked in the shower and her soaping all over his body.

Darn hormones.

'I brought a snack from the house,' she said.

Although it was brilliantly sunny with a bright blue sky, it was a chilly winter's day. When Ned pulled on a thick padded jacket, she was glad he'd covered up all that temptation. As she walked beside him she was careful not to brush against him or have any contact whatsoever. Just in case she acted on erotic impulse instead of reasoned decision.

They headed towards a table and chairs that had been set up for people who might want to watch the action on the arena. It was a beautiful setting with graceful eucalypts planted in stands around the perimeter of the arena, apple trees where the observers sat.

She'd brought some cookies and a flask of coffee from the house for Ned. There was fizzy mineral water for her. She could no longer stomach coffee, which she usually enjoyed— another change caused by pregnancy.

Freya realised it was the first time she had been completely alone with Ned since she'd arrived here. She took the nearest chair. He solicitously tucked a woollen rug around her knees, although she was warmly dressed. He flung himself down on the next chair and poured himself a mug of coffee. 'You're spending quite a bit of time with the horses,' he said. 'When are you going to show me some photos?'

'When I get some that really do the subjects justice,' she said. 'It's quite a learning curve for me.'

'And you're a perfectionist. I have every confidence you'll be brilliant at equine photography. There could be a business in it, you know. Look how you took to garden photography. I've told you how much my mother loved your shoot. Best birthday present I've ever given her, she told me.'

'I'm so pleased to hear that,' she said. She'd put her heart and soul into those photos. To please Ned, she realised, more than his mother.

'By the way, you might be interested to know my father gave her pearl earrings. He's obviously in the know about her birthstone.'

Freya laughed. 'That's cute. Did you see your mum for her birthday?'

'Of course. My parents are still in Italy but I flew out for a quick visit to surprise her. They'll be back in a few weeks.' He paused, put his mug back down on the table. 'You know, they'll be over the moon at the news of another grandchild.'

'You haven't told them, have you?' she said on a surge of panic. They'd agreed to keep the news secret even from his family, until they'd come to terms with what it meant to them both as parents.

'Not yet. But they'll have to know.'

'I realise that.' She sighed. 'This property, the history, your family, they're part of our baby's heritage, aren't they?' All this wealth and privilege and the security and certainty that came with that.

Ned went quiet and Freya realised it was the first time she had said *our* baby.

'Yes, they are,' Ned said, wondering if Freya realised the significance of what she'd just said. Up until now it had been *her* baby. 'And it's a wonderful heritage. Perhaps our child will be riding a pony on this very arena in a few years' time.'

'How old were you when you first got on a horse?'

'I'm told I begged to get up on horseback as soon as I could walk. By eighteen months I was being led on a miniature pony. I could ride her by myself when I was four. Strictly supervised, of course.'

'Do you think you're *born* a horse person?'

'I think *I* was born that way, but you can come to it at any age. Why do you ask?' He held his breath for her answer.

'I've never had anything to do with horses. But I'm fascinated by yours. They're so beautiful and I… I find myself wanting to be around them.'

Just the answer he wanted to hear.

Common ground at last.

'Do you think you'd ever want to ride one?'

She nodded. 'I actually think I would. A small, gentle one, that is. I watch you and think it must be an incredible feeling, to be in a partnership with the horse you're riding.'

'I could teach you,' he said. 'After the—'

'Baby is born,' she finished for him. 'Maybe.'

She wasn't going to commit to anything. He paused, cautious about where he wanted to take the conversation. 'Why do you dislike the country so much?'

She paused. 'You know, I've started to wonder that myself? I think it's because I've never actually spent time in the country. It's the unknown and…and I'm frightened of the unknown.'

Ned remembered how when Wil had first come here, he hadn't been able to sleep because it was so quiet and dark and he'd found the sounds of animals scary. Wil's aim had been to hitch a ride on a truck and run far away to live life on his own at age thirteen. He'd been a bird with broken wings too. Until Five and a Half Mile Creek and the love of his adoptive family had worked their magic on him. Ned wanted that magic for Freya too.

'Could it be that you fear the unknown because you were thrust into unknown territory every time you were placed with a new home? That must have been very scary for a child.'

'It was. So when I finally took charge of my life, I clung to the familiar. You know Richmond is next door to Abbotsford, where I lived with my grandparents? I haven't strayed far. Any time I want to, I can go there and see the house I lived in when they were alive and I had a family. The house is different now, of course, but it's still standing.'

'Could be a kind of security, not necessarily a bad thing. Like a little kid has a blankie. Wil's little Nina has one.'

Freya laughed. 'I'm too old for a blankie.'

But not for kindness and security. Everyone needed those, no matter how old they were. And he ached to give them to her.

'What about you?' she said. 'Why did you hate the city so much?'

'I think it goes back to my childhood.' Though now he realised the disaster of his relationship with Leanne had a lot to do with it too.

'You said you felt like you were in exile when you had to live in Brunswick, which, by the way, is a very cool place.'

He snorted. 'I certainly didn't think so. I felt like a caged animal. I was utterly miserable away from here. I… I think, deep down, I saw being sent to the city as a punishment.'

She frowned. 'Why is that?'

'Even when I was little, I was aware of the tensions between my parents and I'd do my best to try and make it better.'

'The peacemaker, even then.'

He shrugged. 'It didn't work though, did it? I failed. It was my fault Mum and Dad didn't want to stay together. Or that's how it seemed from my childish perspective. I was punished for my failure by being sent to the city. And yet, as my parents saw it, they were passionate people who just needed to sort out their differences—oblivious to the effect it was having on me. I must have been very difficult. I remember poor Hugh and Gordon trying to take me to fun things in town and I wouldn't have a bar of it.'

'You were stubborn even then.'

'Am I stubborn now?'

'Yes. Very.' She paused. 'I think we both are. Neither of us has budged on the barriers we think make a relationship between us impossible.'

'Except for the no-kids thing.'

'By accident, not design,' she reminded him.

'A happy accident.'

She smiled at that but then sobered again. 'We haven't considered any compromise. But, the way I see it, that compromise would be one-sided. You won't budge from your country life, I'd have to be the one to move here.'

'I've been thinking about that.'

Her brows rose. 'Really?'

'That surprises you?'

'Frankly, it does. That condition seemed non-negotiable.'

He turned in his chair so he faced her directly. 'You said something, that last visit, about how you were worried you wouldn't make a good mother because you had been neglected by your own mother.'

'I remember. Since then I've thought about that a lot. Now that I'm actually going to be a mother myself, I realise I did have a mother's love. Only it was from my grandmother. Also, I'm a very different person from my mother. I'm twenty-eight, not seventeen. I've got a career. Savings. And—'

'And, don't forget, the baby has a fantastic father who wants to be part of its life.'

'I was coming to that.' She smiled, her eyes sparkling. 'Our baby does indeed have a fantastic father.' She had been studiously avoiding his touch, but when he took her hand, encased now in a fine-knitted purple wool glove, she held it tight as if she didn't want to let him go.

'And a fantastic mother. I have no doubt about that.'

She looked down to her lap, didn't meet his gaze. 'I'm sorry about…about the way I handled the pregnancy. I should have told you as soon as I knew. It was just such a shock. Then I got so ill. And we'd parted so finally and I thought—'

'I know what you thought and we've sorted that now. But there's something I still have to sort. Let me get back to what I started to say. You were worried about the influence on you of your rather tragic young mother. Now think about my parents.'

She looked up. 'Well, I don't actually know them so I can't—'

'Why didn't I see it before? A creative young woman with a successful career comes out here to work her design magic on the house. Falls for the farmer who owns the place. She gives up her life in the city to move out to a place she thinks is—'

'Too far from civilisation,' Freya said.

'See the parallels?'

'I'm beginning to,' she said slowly.

'The wife is miserable. Her husband is out on the land all day. She misses her career, the stimulus of the city. They don't get the big family she'd hoped for, just one little boy. But her husband refuses to spend more time than he absolutely has to in Melbourne. Even though they own a mansion in Toorak and he's wealthy enough to employ a manager. He finally makes a compromise but not before he nearly loses his wife and son.'

'Replace *interior designer* with *photographer*. History repeats itself.'

He shook his head slowly to emphasise his point. 'Only you didn't let it. You called it quits and went back. The city girl with the purple hair saw sense, while the practical, steady farmer stayed blind to it.'

'True. But the irony is, the more I'm here, the more I love it. I'm beginning to think I could be happy living in the country. Not all the time, but some of the time.'

'Are you serious?'

'Surprisingly, yes. Your cousin Erin called in yesterday afternoon. From the sound of it, people out here have quite an active social life. I had no idea.'

'They do. We have to make our own fun but country life can be very social. Being able to ride a horse helps.'

'So Erin said. I liked her a lot, by the way. We're already friends.'

'Why didn't you tell me she was here?'

'She asked me not to.'

He frowned. 'And why would that be? I love her, but my cousin has a habit of putting her oar in where it's not wanted.'

'Well…'

'What did she say?'

'She told me to put you out of your misery and marry you.'

'What?'

'There's more. She said you obviously adore me and you'll be the world's best father.'

'How did she—? Did you tell her—?'

'She told me she breeds horses and she can always tell when a mare is in foal. And that she was clearly looking at a woman in the early stages of pregnancy.'

Ned fumed. Erin had better not have said anything to Freya about him having been *five times a groomsman and never a groom.* 'I'll have words with her.'

'Actually it was quite funny. She compared me to a brood mare—she actually used that term—you compared me to a sheep. What is it with you country folk?'

'We're well meaning,' he said. 'But maybe we need to get to the city more.'

'It might help,' she said with a laugh.

'Freya, I say that in jest but I mean it. Why do we have to be city girl and country boy? Why can't we each be both city and country?'

* * *

Freya stared at him. Her heart started to pound so loudly she was sure Ned must hear it. 'I'm not sure what you mean.'

He pushed his chair back but kept his gaze on her. 'I didn't expect to inherit Five and a Half Mile Creek for quite a few years more. Perhaps because I've come to the management of the property sooner rather than later, I've felt I had to prove myself. I've put it ahead of anything else, certainly ahead of my personal life.'

'Understandable,' she said. 'It's an immense responsibility.'

What was he trying to say?

'Then you tootled up the driveway in that little purple van, like something out of a story book, and—*wham*—turned my life upside down.'

'Did I?' she said.

He smiled. 'You know you did.' He reached out and brushed his fingers through her hair, sending shivers of awareness through her.

The first time he'd touched her since she'd been back.

'By the way, what's happened to your purple stripe? It's fading.'

'I'm being really careful what I eat and what I put in my body, and that includes hair-dye chemicals.'

'Pity. I like it. Promise you'll dye it again after the baby is born?'

'I… I promise.' She would do it for herself, not because it pleased him, she told herself. Heck, she'd do it for him if he found it pleasing. 'So you were saying about the city and country thing?'

'I'm not genetically completely country,' he said. 'As I've told you, there are things I like about city life too. Music in particular—jazz, classical concerts, rock concerts. Seeing your great little apartment made me remember how much fun I'd had there.' He frowned with concentration as he worked his way through his thoughts.

She leaned closer. 'What exactly are you trying to say, Ned?'

'That my life doesn't have to be strictly in the country. Neither does yours.'

'You mean it could be both?'

'We could live between here and the Toorak apartment. You liked it, didn't you?'

'It's fabulous. Although I would like to see

it more warm and welcoming—a home, not a showcase.'

'You could keep up your career.'

'Your mother going off to Melbourne didn't work for your parents.'

He shook his head. 'I'm not talking about that kind of arrangement where you go back to the city by yourself for weeks on end. We'd go together. No separations.'

'But your work?'

'A lot of my work is behind a desk anyway and could be done as well in Toorak as it is here. My managers already do most of the hands-on work so I don't really need to do as much as I do.'

'But you do it because you like it. Wouldn't you miss it?'

'I'd miss you more,' he said slowly.

She squeezed his hand tightly, almost too overcome to speak. 'Th...thank you.'

'We could cut down on the travelling time by flying. You've seen how easy it is to fly by helicopter. We have a light plane too. You could get your pilot's licence if you wanted.'

Her, a pilot? Why not? 'You've really thought about this.'

His mouth twisted. 'I've had a lot of time on my own to think.'

Ned.

She hated to think of him being on his own. She put the hand he wasn't holding on his cheek and, for a long, still moment, looked into his eyes. What she saw there made her heart turn over.

She let her hand drop. 'It makes sense,' she said, excitement starting to fizz and spark.

'One more thing. I didn't like boarding school. As I suspect we're both family folk at heart, our child might not like it either.'

She shuddered at her ever-present memories of her disrupted childhood. 'You could be right about that.' No way would her child ever be treated as she had been.

'Our schedules might be determined by term time as well as by seasonal farming events. Elementary school at our nearest town, Hill-top—'

'You'd send your child to a state school?' That surprised her.

'I went there—my parents thought it important. It's where you form friendships that are important out here where families are far-flung. But there isn't a high school, so that would be a private school in Melbourne. What do you think?'

'It sounds rather wonderful, a perfect compromise, in fact. But I—'

He put up his hand again. 'You don't have to say anything. I've dumped a lot on you. I just want you to think that the compromise doesn't have to be one-sided. And that I really want to be a good father to our child.'

Freya was so tightly wrapped in the rug, that she struggled to get out of her chair. Ned laughed and pulled her to her feet. Then she was in his arms, and they were kissing as if it hadn't been more than two months since their last kiss. How she'd missed his kisses, his hugs, *him*.

She felt instantly aroused and wondered if the hay stacked in the barn would make a good spot to make love. But no, that would be too scandalous. Later, perhaps, when there was no one else around, it could be fun though.

'Ned, you're right. We do need to think about this. But the way my thoughts are going, I... I suggest you ask me again to marry you fairly soon.'

'Or you could ask me.'

'I find myself feeling surprisingly traditional about this. It has to be you doing the proposing.'

'I'll come up with something special,' he said with his endearing grin.

'In the meantime, I have a complaint about the guest room.'

'I'll get onto Marian, I—'

She put her finger across his lips. 'It's not something Marian can fix. You see, the bed is too big and too lonely without you...'

He placed his hand on her tummy for the first time, and she thrilled to the protective gesture. 'Is it okay to, uh...you know...when you're pregnant?'

'Please don't tell me what the situation is with brood mares. But my doctor says it's perfectly okay to make love. I say, the sooner the better.'

'You don't hear me complaining,' he said as he put his arm around her and walked her towards the house.

CHAPTER THIRTEEN

NEXT MORNING, WORKING on her laptop, Freya scrolled through the photos of Ned riding Hero she had taken the day before. They were good, really good. She had captured the speed, agility and power of the man on horseback but also the intensity of the communication between man and animal.

That both Ned and his very valuable horse were extremely good-looking did help. But it was the spirit of the images that made her catch her breath. She loved her work as a commercial photographer but had always wanted to work artistically too, perhaps towards an exhibition. Maybe this change in her life marked more exciting new directions than she had imagined.

She lingered on one image where Ned was looking straight at the camera and grinning at her. It wasn't the most artistic of the shots but she loved it.

She loved him.

She had fought hard against falling in love with Ned, but it had been a losing battle. In another parallel with his parents' story, she had fallen for the boss of Five and a Half Mile Creek. She wouldn't go so far as to say love at first sight, although she couldn't actually pinpoint the moment. Ned with his kindness and strength and—yes—hotness had breached the barriers around her heart.

Today, Ned was going to propose again, and this time she would accept without hesitation. There was no reason not to. She loved him and she was pregnant with his baby. A baby who she would make sure had a much better childhood than she'd had. Not in terms of material wealth, although there appeared to be that in spades. But to be born to happily married parents was a great gift. Parents who loved each other.

Ned hadn't actually said he loved her but then she hadn't told him how she felt either. Not with words, anyway. Yesterday, she'd been surprised when he hadn't responded when she'd told him his cousin Erin had said he adored her—either to confirm or deny it.

But she didn't doubt that she loved him and she would let him know that in both words and actions.

She was working in the room that had originally been Ned's mother's design studio. As soon as he'd brought her here last week, Ned had allocated it to her as her personal space. His study was next door. She loved this room as much as she loved his study. The light was perfect, and it opened out onto one of her favourite parts of the garden.

The winter garden had its own stark beauty. Although many of the shrubs and trees had lost their leaves, there were big, fat red rosehips on most of the roses. Pansies and hellebores gave patches of subtle colour in mauves and pinks and purples. She would like to document every season in this garden. Perhaps she could even get interested in gardening. Possibly it was something she could bond over with her future mother-in-law.

Last night, after Ned had gone to sleep—the joy of knowing she would sleep in his arms every night of their lives!—she had thought about the wider implications of marrying Ned. She would gain a new family. Her baby would be born into a family of loving parents, grand-parents, numerous cousins and an uncle and aunt. When she finally reunited with Wil and met Georgia it would be as their sister-in-law. How wonderfully that had turned out.

Before she settled back to her screen, she patted Molly on the head where she lay at her feet. It had been unnerving—and at first a little frightening—the way Ned's dog had at-tached herself to Freya on her return to Five and a Half Mile Creek.

Ned said Molly had appointed herself as Freya's protector. Maybe the old dog instinc-tively knew she carried her beloved master's child. After all, she'd had pups of her own. At first, Freya had shooed her away but Molly had been persistent. Once Freya had lost her fear, she had come to welcome the sweet ani-mal's company. And Molly was very coopera-tive about having her photo taken.

Freya bent her head again to culling the im-ages of yesterday's shoot. So many to pick from. She paused at one where Ned's head was angled as if he was listening to what Hero had to say to him about the manoeuvre they were making. Ned would love it. In fact it was such a good shot she decided to print it out to show him. It could actually be worthy of framing.

There was a printer in Ned's office. She'd already used it so the link was in her laptop. No need to disturb Ned down at the admin building. Besides, she wanted it to be a surprise.

She went next door into Ned's office, accompanied by Molly, her claws clicking companionably on the wooden floor.

Ned's computer stood quietly on his desk. As she hunted for photographic paper, she accidentally knocked his mouse and his screen brightened into life.

She would never snoop. But she couldn't escape the image on the screen. It was a personal page on one of the big dating sites.

Ned's page.

Her mouth dried. What was this doing open? There was a nice enough photo of Ned, though she could do a lot better—he looked a bit self-conscious. And there…there was his profile with a list of requirements for his ideal wife.

Freya felt the blood drain from her face and she had to hang onto the edge of his desk for support as she read the particulars of Ned's ideal wife.

1. Genuine enjoyment of country life essential.
2. Management experience to help run the business would be advantageous. Accountant or lawyer ideal.
3. Love of animals, particularly horses. A vet or vet nurse would be very welcome.
4. An interest in gardening.
5. A good cook.
6. Conservative, country-focused values.

What a pompous list. Nausea rose in her throat. She didn't meet one of his requirements. Not one. The gardening was only a new possibility. No wonder he wanted to encourage her interest in horses. Freya cursed a long string of the impressive curse words she had learned during her time in care. Molly whimpered, aware of her distress.

Ned hadn't out-and-out asked for a woman with child-bearing hips but that requirement was implicit in the rest of his requirements. She was ahead of the game there, she thought cynically.

She was bearing his child, the heir to Five and a Half Mile Creek and a fortune. That heir would need to be legitimate. He'd actually told her that Hudson children were not born out of 'wedlock'. Of course he wanted to get married to legitimise his offspring—no matter how unsuitable the mother was as a wife. And then what for her? Find herself discarded and facing a custody battle she'd never be able to afford to fight?

How could she have got him so wrong?

Her first instinct was to run away, back to her apartment in Melbourne. But Ned had driven her here and she had no means of escape. Her van was parked back at the studio.

Again, she was trapped. Only this time she didn't feel horror at being trapped, rather an intense wave of sadness, because she had been beginning to think of Five and a Half Mile Creek as home. And Ned as the man for her.

Freya dragged her feet out into the hallway and back to the studio. There was an elegant, comfortable armchair that faced the view of the garden. She had already pinpointed it as a perfect chair to sit in while breastfeeding her baby.

Now she flopped into it, exhausted, shaken, *betrayed*. Molly gave a huge doggy sigh, circled, lay down and rested her head on Freya's feet. Freya closed her eyes against her frantic, anguished thoughts and tried to make sense of her future.

Because it couldn't be here.

It wasn't every day a guy got to propose to the woman he loved. Ned was on such a high, he was whistling the tune of Mendelssohn's *Wedding March* as he strode along the corridor to his study. For some sentimental reason, he wanted to be holding his lucky horseshoe when he asked Freya to be his wife.

He headed to where the horseshoe was propped, ends up as it should be, and stopped suddenly. Odd that his computer monitor should be on; even odder that Freya's laptop was on his desk. He went to move her laptop, accidentally nudged his keyboard, and his screen lit up.

Hell.

Stricken, he stared at the screen. That stupid list on that stupid dating site.

Freya had seen it.

Who knew what conclusions she might have drawn? He cursed long and loud.

Ned picked up his horseshoe—he really had need of it now—put it in his pocket, and headed into Freya's studio.

She was lying back in the armchair, with Molly stretched out by her feet. For a moment, he watched her. Freya's eyes were closed but Ned wasn't convinced she was asleep. Her breathing pattern didn't seem authentic. Molly looked up at him, thumped her tail in greeting. He liked how his dog was so protective of Freya and was relieved Molly didn't growl at him for hurting her new mistress.

Because Freya must be hurt. Really hurt. And who could blame her? No wonder she didn't want to open her eyes.

Ned squatted down on his haunches next to the chair, where he could look directly into her face. 'Freya? Are you awake?' A suspicious flickering of her eyelashes, but no reply. 'Blink once if you hate me.' A definite blink. As to be expected. 'So you're not talking to me?' Another blink.

'I won't even ask if you think I'm the stupidest guy on earth. Because you'll wear your eyelids out blinking your agreement.' No blink.

'The dating site. I never used it. Not once. But the subscription came up for renewal and I had the page open to cancel it. I forgot to close it down.' Inwardly he groaned. 'That list.' Her mouth tightened. 'I wrote it after Wil and Georgia's wedding. I was so happy for them but it made me realise how lonely I was. How much I wanted a wife and family of my own. Your new friend, my cousin Erin, wouldn't stop teasing me about my single status. But it's impossible to meet anyone out here you haven't known all your life. A dating site seemed a reasonable option.'

He paused. 'Are you listening? I don't want to be giving this speech for Molly's benefit. Two blinks if you're listening to me.' Two blinks.

'Okay. I'll continue my spiel, which, by the way, I'm finding quite humiliating.' Was that a slight upward curve of her mouth? 'I hadn't had a lot of luck with love, right back to schooldays and Teresita. Then there was the disaster with Leanne. The list was more a defensive thing, really. I didn't dare put down into writing that I'd decided…that…that love hurt too much for me to pursue. I could do without it. Still listening?' Blink.

'Then along you came. And with you came something I had never imagined. I was enchanted with you from the second I met you.' He paused. 'Can you please open your eyes? Maybe talk to me. I'm really sorry you saw that list. Gutted in fact. But it means nothing.'

Slowly Freya's eyes opened. They were wary and tear-stained. The sight wrenched at his heart. He hated to see her hurt, to know that *he* had hurt her. Slowly, she sat up straight and swivelled to face him. Now it seemed he was kneeling in supplication before her—which seemed entirely appropriate.

'I don't meet one criterion on your list.' Her voice broke. 'Not one.'

'They were stupid criteria for a wife.'

'They read more like an ad for a housekeeping manager.'

Ned winced.

'I expect she would have come wielding a stock whip,' Freya said.

'I'm impressed you know what a stock whip is. You're really turning into a country girl.'

'Ned,' she said warningly. 'Don't push it. You're lucky I'm even hearing you out.'

'I know. And I've got a new wife wish-list.'

She frowned. 'I don't know what you mean.'

'It's much shorter than the old one. Do you want to hear it?'

She blinked.

He grinned. And held on tight to his lucky horseshoe.

'I haven't written the list down, but I'll pretend I'm reading it out. Try not to interrupt me.'

'Okay,' she said.

He thought on his feet—or rather on his knees. 'One. Must make me laugh and help me not to take myself so seriously. Two. Must love the colour purple. Three. Must accept that she is loved from the depths of his heart by her husband-to-be. Four. Must be named Freya Delaney.'

He was suddenly too choked up to think of any more.

Freya leaned towards him, her eyes glistening. 'I think I might fit those criteria.'

Ned got to his feet and pulled her up from her chair to look at him. He cupped her face in his hands—her lovely face that had become so utterly precious to him. 'Does that mean you'll do me the honour of becoming my wife?'

'Do you want me to blink or say *yes*?'

He laughed. 'Please say *yes*.'

'Yes,' she said immediately. Then blinked as well. 'Nothing would make me happier than to be your wife.'

He kissed her, long and sweet and tenderly. 'I love you, Freya.'

'I love you, too, Ned. From…from the depths of my heart.'

He took her left hand in his, and held it up. 'I haven't got you a ring.'

'I don't expect…'

'There's a safe in the next room containing a collection of family jewellery. Wil gave Georgia our grandmother's emerald ring. I can have my choice of ring for my bride. But I would rather you designed your own engagement ring, unique to you. I thought…amethyst and diamonds.'

Her smile wobbled at the edges. 'Of course I would prefer that, Ned. You know me so well already.'

'I felt I knew you as soon as I met you.'

'I had the same feeling,' she said. 'As if…as if we were meant to be.'

'Your ring will have nothing to do with the past, just our present.'

'And our future, Ned,' she said, rising on tiptoe to kiss him. 'Our wonderful, wonderful future.'

EPILOGUE

Six weeks later

BECAUSE FREYA HAD never intended to marry, she'd never thought much about weddings. But her wonderful Ned loved weddings and all that went with them.

Ned had been a groomsman five times and was—by her own definition—the marrying kind. As soon as they'd got engaged, he'd been full of plans for a traditional wedding in the country town church where generations of his family had wed. Because she loved him, and in the spirit of compromise they intended to follow in their life together, Freya had agreed to a church wedding.

But she'd cringed at the idea of a formal ceremony, held in a church packed with guests she didn't know and who didn't know her. Ned, however, wanted to celebrate their marriage in the company of his family, his many friends, and all the Five and a Half Mile Creek employees, in the Hudson family tradition.

Again she and Ned had compromised and agreed to an intimate, family-only wedding in the church, followed the next day by a big party for everyone at Five and a Half Mile Creek. There, Ned could proudly introduce Freya as his wife to the greater community.

So now Freya stood in the vestibule of the flower-bedecked church, ready to make her walk down the aisle towards Ned, where he waited for her with his best man, Wil, and his father. His parents, Jackie and Dave, had flown back from Italy for the wedding and Freya and Ned had wanted them to be part of the ceremony.

First down the aisle was tiny Nina, Wil and Georgia's toddler daughter, determined to show off her new-found walking skills, looking adorable in a flouncy white dress with a huge bow at the back and cute little satin shoes. Freya couldn't help but wonder if she might have a little girl, or a little boy like Ned. Her heart swelled at the thought. Either would be loved.

Halfway down the aisle, Nina tired and sat down on her bottom. Amid fond laughter from everyone else, the littlest attendant was then swept up in the arms of her mother, dark-haired Georgia, who, holding her daughter, continued down the aisle. She was followed by Ned's cousin, red-haired Erin. Both bridesmaids wore simple long gowns in different shades of lavender and carried purple iris. Jackie was next, in an elegant purple silk suit she'd bought in Italy for the wedding. Freya had warmed to her future mother-in-law the minute she'd met her, and they were already close. Ned's father had welcomed her with a big hug and had taken it upon himself to school her in all things country and the history of the Hudson family.

Once all the attendants reached the altar, the organist—Ned had insisted on an organist—struck up the wedding march processional and Freya prepared to walk down the aisle. She'd thought she'd be nervous, but she wasn't. She was exhilarated and excited about taking her place next to Ned.

'Ready?' asked Hugh.

'Looking forward to it,' she said.

Both Hugh and burly, bearded Gordon were accompanying her down the aisle. Not to 'give her away'—she didn't agree with that part of the ceremony—but to represent her family. The two men weren't family by blood, but they were family of the heart to not only her but also Ned.

Family.

She had longed for it since she'd lost her nanna and now she had found her place with Ned and his family. A week ago, she'd reunited with Wil to find the bond of friendship still strong after all those intervening years. She'd made another friend in his wife. Georgia had sobbed with joy that her husband had met again the girl who'd been one of his very few friends in a dark childhood, and who was now marrying his beloved brother.

'Let's go,' Freya said to her escorts, as she looked ahead to where Ned waited for her. He looked very handsome in a morning suit. She had to force herself to step sedately as she made her way up the aisle, when what she wanted to do was lift up the skirts of her long gown and run to him.

* * *

As Ned stood at the altar with his brother and father by his side, he realised Freya had been absolutely right to keep their wedding ceremony simple and limited to the people who were closest to them. The warmth of his inclusive family—who had embraced her with love and welcome—had already worked magic on his beautiful Freya, who was learning to trust and love in return. And their baby would be born into that caring circle.

Now he watched, with hammering heart and dry mouth, the exquisite vision floating her way up the aisle towards him. She was wearing an elegant, full-skirted white dress with long, tight sleeves—flattering on her newly rounded figure. A voluminous white veil trailed behind her.

More wings to bring her to him.

Purple and white flowers were twisted through her hair and in her bouquet.

'She's lovely, Ned, in every way,' Wil said to him, in a low voice. 'I can't tell you how happy I am that you and Freya are getting married. When we were kids, I wanted Tegan for a sister. Now she finally will be.'

'I've thanked you in my head, so many times, for rescuing her from that dangerous situation.' Ned spoke to Wil but he couldn't keep his eyes off Freya.

'Now she has you to look out for her,' said Wil. 'Things couldn't have worked out better, could they? It's as if it was fated to be.'

'You could say that,' Ned said, watching as his bride moved nearer. That first day he'd thought Freya had floated in from the rose garden on fairy wings. She'd proved to be only too earthy and real and he loved her all the more for it.

As Freya and her escorts moved closer, Ned noticed another one of the curiously smug glances between Hugh and his mother. Earlier, he'd even caught them in a self-congratulatory fist-bump. Something about that exchange made him wonder why the house had needed photographing at all, when his mother was retired.

Then all he could think about was Freya, as Hugh handed her to him and he took her hand in his to draw her close. 'Hello, soon-to-be-wife,' he murmured.

'Hello, soon-to-be-husband,' she whispered,

with the lovely, gap-toothed smile that had entranced him from the beginning, her eyes luminous with love. 'Do you have your lucky horseshoe in your pocket?'

'All ready to catch our good luck.'

As they stood facing each other in front of the priest, their family members stood close by, as if they, too, were making vows— pledging to help support the young couple on their journey into marriage and parenthood and a lifetime of love.

His beloved Freya, who'd said she would never marry but was marrying him; who never wanted to have children but was carrying his baby; repeated her vows in in a clear, steady voice that rang with sincerity and commitment. He was so overcome with emotion that he choked out the words, although he hoped with equal sincerity. But he didn't stumble as he slipped the simple platinum wedding band next to the amethyst-and-diamond ring already on the third finger of her left hand, then held his hand steady as Freya slipped a matching band onto his ring finger.

'I now pronounce you man and wife,' proclaimed the priest.

Ned had never heard such wonderful words. 'I love you, wife,' he said.

'I love you, dearest husband,' she murmured back. 'For ever and for always.'

Ned didn't wait for anyone to give him permission to kiss his bride, but pulled her to him and claimed her mouth with his. She wound her arms around his neck and kissed him back and they kissed and kissed to the accompaniment of cheering and clapping. They only pulled away, laughing and joyous, to accept heartfelt congratulations and well wishes for their new life together.

* * * * *

LET'S TALK
Romance

For exclusive extracts, competitions
and special offers, find us online:

- facebook.com/millsandboon
- @millsandboonuk
- @millsandboon

Or get in touch on 0844 844 1351*

For all the latest titles coming soon,
visit millsandboon.co.uk/nextmonth

Want even more
ROMANCE?

Join our bookclub today!

'Mills & Boon books, the perfect way to escape for an hour or so.'

Miss W. Dyer

'Excellent service, promptly delivered and very good subscription choices.'

Miss A. Pearson

'You get fantastic special offers and the chance to get books before they hit the shops'

Mrs V. Hall

Visit millsandbook.co.uk/Bookclub and save on brand new books.

MILLS & BOON